OUR CANADIAN Girl

OUR
CANADIAN
Girl

Treasury Volume One

Lynne Kositsky

Kathy Stinson

Julie Lawson

Sharon E. McKay

VIKING
CANADA

VIKING CANADA

Penguin Group (Canada), a division of Pearson Penguin Canada Inc.,
10 Alcorn Avenue, Toronto, Ontario M4V 3B2

Penguin Group (U.K.), 80 Strand, London WC2R 0RL, England
Penguin Group (U.S.), 375 Hudson Street, New York, New York 10014, U.S.A.
Penguin Group (Australia) Inc., 250 Camberwell Road, Camberwell, Victoria 3124, Australia
Penguin Group (Ireland), 25 St. Stephen's Green, Dublin 2, Ireland
Penguin Books India (P) Ltd, 11, Community Centre, Panchsheel Park, New Delhi – 110 017, India
Penguin Group (New Zealand), cnr Rosedale and Airborne Roads, Albany, Auckland 1310,
New Zealand
Penguin Books (South Africa) (Pty) Ltd, 24 Sturdee Avenue, Rosebank 2196, South Africa

Penguin Group, Registered Offices: 80 Strand, London WC2R 0RL, England

Rachel: A Mighty Big Imagining; Marie-Claire: Dark Spring; Emily: Across the James Bay Bridge; and
Penelope: Terror in the Harbour first published in Penguin paperback by Penguin Canada, 2001

Published in Viking Canada hardcover by Penguin Group (Canada),
a division of Pearson Penguin Canada Inc., 2003

1 2 3 4 5 6 7 8 9 10   (FR)

Rachel: A Mighty Big Imagining copyright © Lynne Kositsky, 2001
Marie-Claire: Dark Spring copyright © Kathy Stinson, 2001
Emily: Across the James Bay Bridge copyright © Julie Lawson, 2001
Penelope: Terror in the Harbour copyright © Sharon E. McKay, 2001

Rachel: A Mighty Big Imagining interior and cover illustrations © Ron Lightburn, 2001
Marie-Claire: Dark Spring interior and cover illustrations © Sharif Tarabay, 2001
Emily: Across the James Bay Bridge interior and cover illustrations © Janet Wilson, 2001
Penelope: Terror in the Harbour interior and cover illustrations © Ron Lightburn, 2001
Cover design: Cathy MacLean
Interior design: Matthews Communications Design Inc.
Map: Sharon Matthews

*Publisher's note: This book is a work of fiction. Names, characters, places and incidents either
are the product of the authors' imagination or are used fictitiously, and any resemblance
to actual persons living or dead, events, or locales is entirely coincidental.*

Manufactured in Canada.

NATIONAL LIBRARY OF CANADA CATALOGUING IN PUBLICATION

Our Canadian girl treasury.

ISBN 0-670-04484-9 (v. 1)

1. Canada—History—Juvenile fiction.

PS8329.O87   2003   jC813'.54   C2003-905665-1

Visit the Penguin Group (Canada) website at **www.penguin.ca**

Dear Reader,

Welcome to Our Canadian Girl, a series of historical fiction for kids! When Penguin first decided to create this series, we thought about the books that we loved to read when we were kids. It was always fun and interesting to read about kids from different places and times in Canadian history, and imagine ourselves in their places. What was a typical day for a French-Canadian girl in Montreal in the 1880s? What would be the best birthday present to receive in 1890? What would it have been like to be a child of slaves during the American Revolution, freed to start a new life in Nova Scotia? What might you have been doing in Halifax on the morning of the great explosion in 1917? In Our Canadian Girl, you'll read about all of this and so much more!

In this, our first treasury, you will meet four spirited girls who come from different places and

*times in Canadian history, each of whom meets
some ordinary—and extraordinary—challenges
in her day-to-day life. In the first story,* A
Mighty Big Imagining, *you'll meet Rachel,
who in 1783 boards a ship with her mother that
will take them from a life of slavery in America
to a life of promised freedom in Nova Scotia.
In the second story,* Dark Spring, *young
Marie-Claire faces the everyday challenges of
life in Montreal in 1885 as a smallpox epidemic
sweeps the city. Ten years later and across the
continent in Victoria, B.C., Emily's relationship
with her family's servant, Hing, leads her to
discover the vibrant and mysterious world of
Chinatown in* Across the James Bay Bridge.
And we end with Terror in the Harbour,
*the story of Penny, a young girl whose world is
changed forever one cold December morning in
1917, when two ships collide in Halifax Harbour.*

*As different as all of these girls are, they also
have much in common. They are—each in her
own way—smart, strong, and brave.*

*I hope you'll enjoy these stories. If so, you'll
be happy to learn that there are many more
stories of these and other Canadian girls. At*

the front of this book, you'll find a list of all the other Our Canadian Girl stories available to you at your local library and bookstore.

Happy reading!

Yours,

Barbara Berson
Editor, Our Canadian Girl

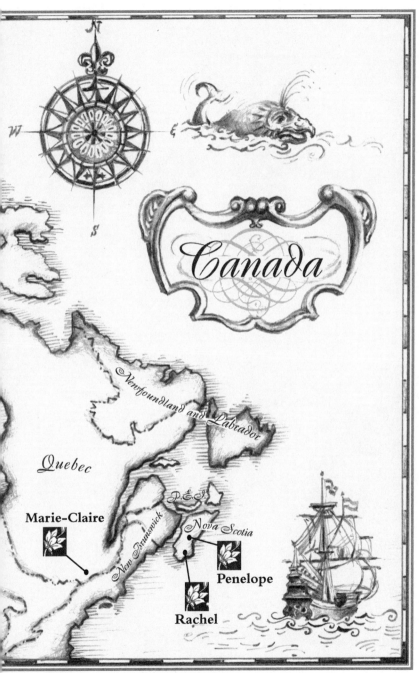

N

W   S

Canada

Newfoundland and Labrador

Quebec

Marie-Claire

P.E.I.

New Brunswick

Nova Scotia

Penelope

Rachel

 Marks the locations of the stories

CONTENTS

RACHEL: BOOK ONE

A MIGHTY BIG
IMAGINING

LYNNE KOSITSKY

For my children

MEET RACHEL

I T IS HARD ENOUGH TO IMAGINE LIFE WITHOUT TV, electricity, or running water. Now try to picture living without enough food or clothing, without a comfortable home or medicine. This is the world that Rachel, a slave girl of the eighteenth century, was born into.

Rachel grew up near Charlestown, in South Carolina, where at least two-thirds of the population were slaves. Rachel's grandmother was kidnapped by slave traders and brought over from West Africa, together with many other black people. All were forced to stay in the British colony, living in terrible conditions.

The year our story takes place is 1783, and most of the descendants of these original slaves now work in the rice fields of the plantations, planting and picking the rice known as "Carolina gold." It's a harsh and thankless life, and many die before their time.

In a sense Rachel and her mother were lucky during their years on the plantation. They were house slaves and did not have to work outside in the searing heat. But although the master and mistress were wealthy, with beautiful clothes and sumptuous food, Rachel was dressed in thin rags made of a poor cloth reserved for slaves, and was only ever given rice to eat, the spoiled or broken grains that were not good enough to sell. If she became sick on this diet, she could only get better or die. The master and mistress did not want to spend money on doctors for slaves because they were easily replaced. The mistress was also quick to punish Rachel with a severe beating if she misbehaved.

While Rachel was still a very small child, tension between Britain and her thirteen American colonies grew. The colonists, including Rachel's master, were angry that they were being taxed so heavily, and that Britain had so much control over them. In 1776, after several small clashes, a war called the American Revolution broke out between the colonies and Britain. Almost everybody took sides. Rachel's master supported the Revolution. He was called a Patriot. But some people, the Loyalists, remained loyal to Britain and the English king. They fought on the side of the British army and if caught would often be subjected to the humiliating and dangerous punishment of being covered in hot tar and feathers.

The slaves on Rachel's plantation were caught in the middle. But the British promised them their freedom if they escaped their Patriot owners and fought as Loyalists. Rachel, her mother, and her stepfather decided to run away to the British, and although they did not engage in the fighting, they worked with the soldiers and their wives, setting up camps, cooking, sewing, and washing. When the British lost the war, Rachel's family were afraid that they would be sent back to their owners. The British, however, offered them certificates to show they were free.

By the late fall of 1783, Rachel's stepfather has already been shipped from the port of New York to another British colony, Nova Scotia, while Rachel and her mother wait at the docks, eager to join him.

R UN AWAY from my plantation, near Charlestown by the Cooper River. Three Negroes, my property, going by the names of Titan, Sukey, and Rachel. All speak good English.

Titan, a pretty tall fellow with two toes missing had on when he went away Negro cloth jacket and britches.

Sukey, a thin woman with a scar on the left forehead, had on Negro cloth dress and loose shoes.

Rachel, a very black young girl, straight limbed, daughter of Sukey, had on Negro cloth skirt, shift, no shoes. Took their blankets with them, and an axe. It is thought they may try to join up with the King's forces.

Whoever delivers the said Negroes, any or all of them, to me, Joshua Roberts, at my plantation, or to the work-house at Charlestown, shall receive Ten Pounds currency reward for the fellow, Five Pounds for the woman, Three Pounds for the girl.

"Boats are bad," Mamma had always said. "They take you from your own place, where you belong, to a country far, far across the sea where you mus' slave for a cruel white missus and massa." All the more remarkable, then, that Mamma and Rachel were now standing on the deck of a great ship in the New York harbour, wishing to sail away on it.

"Name?" the Englishman in charge demanded of Mamma. Seated at a desk in the middle of the scrubbed deck, he stared at her quizzically before dipping his quill in ink and holding it poised above his book.

Mamma grasped Rachel's wrist so hard her icy fingers left a pale fingerprint bracelet on her daughter's dark skin. It looked as though she were afraid that Rachel, if released, might run away. But Rachel knew better. Mamma, usually so brave and so bossy, was scared as a cat-trapped mouse and grabbing hold of her for comfort. Mamma was terrified of white people.

"Name?" the man repeated, clearly annoyed.

Rachel glanced behind her. There were at least forty more Negroes waiting in line behind them, thinly clothed and almost dancing with cold on the wind-swept deck. This man probably wanted to be through with his accounting of them so he could get to his hot meal and bed.

"Sukey, suh. And this here's my daughter Rachel."

"Sukey what?"

"Don' have no last name, suh," Mamma mumbled, staring down at the tummy bump of her soon-to-be baby. She was still clutching Rachel's wrist for dear life.

"Were you slaves?"

"Yessuh, the both of us, at Massa Roberts' rice plantation near Charlestown."

"You can take his surname, then. I'll put you down as Sukey and Rachel Roberts." He wrote rapidly.

A little brown bird landed on the deck and hopped towards Rachel.

"If you please, suh . . ." murmured Rachel. She could just make out a very large R and very small O on the yellow paper. Although she couldn't read, she knew the shapes of some of the letters. She'd seen the missus write in her journal often enough.

"Yes, what is it?"

"We don't want his name. He never did anything for us. He only whipped us and called us bad Nigras. We don't want any reminders of him at all. If it please you . . ."

"Well?" A tiny teardrop of ink splashed from the man's waiting pen onto the page.

Rachel glanced at the bird before saying firmly, "Our name is Sparrow. Sukey and Rachel Sparrow."

Mamma sighed in surprise.

"Sparrow be it, then." The man crossed out the R and O and wrote something else in their place. Rachel watched intently. Tossing back his mane of white hair, the man looked at her properly for the first time, as if she were a grown-up. "Your ages?"

"I'm around ten, I'm almost sure. I remember the siege of Charlestown, the terrible noise and fear of it. And Mamma's going on thirty."

"You speak very good English, girl." The man actually smiled, and his face creased like starched linen.

"I was a house slave, suh. I copied the missus, the way she spoke. Then, when we escaped, I copied the soldiers' wives."

"Good for you." A make-believe iron smoothed out his smile, and he went on with his writing.

"Where we goin', suh?" Mamma asked timidly, afraid to interrupt his work.

"To Shelburne, Port Roseway, in Nova Scotia, woman, to a new, free life. Didn't anybody tell you?"

"Oh, yessuh. I jus' wanted to make sure they were right. You see, my husband, Titan, who works for the army, he's on another boat. He's gone before to put up wood houses for the settlers. We wouldn' want to end up someplace else."

"You shall not, I promise you."

"Can we stay on board tonight, suh? We're afraid to go on shore, afraid the massa will find us and drag us back." That was the talk all over town: the slave owners were coming to claim their property now the war was ended. The scar above Mamma's eyebrow seemed to blaze out now, a lick of crimson paint on her brown skin.

"You may. We'll be turning no one away. We sail on the morning tide."

The man waved his hand to dismiss them and gazed at the ocean till his eyes turned the same glass grey as the winter shimmer of water.

"Sukey and Rachel Sparrow, free Nigras in Nova Scotia," Mamma whispered as they climbed below. She'd let go of Rachel at last. "I jus' love the sound of that. Here's your blanket, girl. Gird it round you to stop your shiverin', and never mind the holes."

Rachel nodded. Free Nigras. She didn't even know what that meant. No massa to yell at her, perhaps, and no missus to pull her hair. If she were really lucky, there might even be enough to eat. She thought of all the food on the missus' table in Charlestown and imagined herself stuffing it into her own hungry mouth. That was a mighty big imagining, and she sighed at the effort, pulling her threadbare blanket round her. It was awfully cold up here. She'd never suffered such cold. Even the wild, wet heat of summer on the plantation, with the mosquitoes stinging her skin raw, was better than this. She began the slippery climb down to the ship's hold, hoping the future would be more to her liking than the past.

CHAPTER N° 2

"When will we be there?" Rachel demanded of Mamma. "Has Titan built a house for us? Will it shelter us from the cold?"

They had left port several days before, escorted by a British warship, but their boat had been becalmed for a long time, swaying and dipping in tiny eddies of water. Rachel had begun to think that she'd never see Nova Scotia. Then the winds had picked up, icy and bitter, and sleet had begun to drive at them in a fierce arc. The sails had filled with gusty air and damp, and the boat had groaned, shaking itself like a giant sea creature. Soon it had begun to move again.

Mamma smiled wanly. She was sick to her stomach from the lurching of the ship and the new baby inside her. "Hush," was all she said. "We'll know when we know, and there ain't no use a-frettin' about it."

"I want to know now. I want this trip to end, and for us to be off the boat."

"Trip is jus' an arm long, you can reach clean across it," declared Mamma in that mysterious way of hers, and there was suddenly no more to be said. No more, that is, until a strange ship was sighted in the distance.

"What's that?" shouted Mamma, her fearful voice flying off into the gale.

"I heard someone say it's a privateer, Mamma, a rebel ship, ready to board us. See how close it comes. At least there's no cargo here that could possibly be worth its while."

"No cargo?" broke in a Negro man who was standing alongside of them. "No cargo, hey?

We're the cargo. It'll take us back south and sell us off as slaves."

Mamma's lips went white as pine ash. Rachel, too, felt the blood wash out of her face. To come so far, only to be dragged back. It was unbearable. But as she cuddled close to Mamma, her chin wobbling, her knees weak as cotton, the British warship protecting them fired one warning shot. Rachel and Mamma jumped back as though hit. The rebel boat came no closer. Instead, it shortened its sails and turned away, facing the wind. Soon, to their relief, they had left it far behind, a speck, then a glint, then nothing on the pale horizon.

Rachel thought she'd never feel entirely safe again.

Two days later they sailed into an eerie fog. It muffled the noise of sea and gulls completely. Every creak and cry of the ship sounded as loud as a pistol crack and set their hearts to hammering again.

When the fog began, ever so slowly, to clear, land, hilly and densely wooded, lay before them.

The tops of the trees were still shawled in mist, which also hung like wispy tassels from branches. The sky was clotted with low cloud. One biggish house, half finished, and a few small huts, mean as slave shacks, freckled the shore. The place looked sulky, miserable. And the warship had vanished, gone on its way.

For a moment Rachel felt really lonely and forlorn. But then she spied Titan waiting with throngs of other Negroes on the lip of the small harbour into which they sailed. Titan was immense, head and shoulders above everyone else. As he came into sight, looming like a great ghost out of the icy gloom, he pulled off his cap and whooped it round in circles to greet them. Mamma squeezed Rachel's hand. She was so thrilled to catch sight of his big familiar face after all these months.

"He's got a new hat . . . an' new trousers too," she cried with delight as he stepped out of the crowd. "This mus' be a rich place and no mistake. There mus' be more to it than what we're seein'."

"This here's Birchtown," sneered one of the deckhands. "What you see is what you get. Shelburne is just around the bay a piece. A prettier little new-town you'll never clap eyes on. But that's for whites. This here's your getting-off place. The Nigra stop, you might say, with emphasis on the 'stop.' Git your bundles together."

Rachel didn't move. It made no difference where they were. Everybody despised Negroes.

"Understand me, girl?"

"Oh, yessuh."

"Then what you staring at?"

"Nothing, suh." She picked up her bundle and balanced it on her head. It contained her blanket and some worsted stockings given to her on the boat.

"Home," thought Rachel. "Like it or not, this is it. I guess I'd better get used to it."

CHAPTER Nº 3

"*Is one of them huts along the shore goin'*
to be our house?" Mamma asked Titan, after
the three of them had greeted one another
thoroughly. Rachel had told Titan of their new
surname, and Mamma had admired his hat.

"Not exactly," he said, hoisting his family's
bundles over his shoulder and drawing Mamma
and Rachel away from the crowds.

Titan told them that he'd met every ship for
the past three months. He must have been
hopeful, thought Rachel, then despairing, of

ever seeing his wife and stepdaughter again. But as always, he didn't have much to say. He never used five words when one would do, never used one when he could get by with silence. Rachel remembered with a shock how close-mouthed he was. She would have to learn him all over again.

"Well, where is our house then?" she asked, glancing around. There was no place for a home, surely, not in this mess of forest and great grey boulders.

Titan said nothing, just turned and loped up the nearest hill, his long, badly worn shoes making no mark on the uneven, frosty ground. He couldn't run because of his missing toes, but he sure could walk fast. Mamma and Rachel had a hard time keeping up with him.

Rachel still felt just as dizzy as she'd been on the boat, with the land refusing to stay in place. It wobbled and rose up under her feet, almost tripping her. "I need to get my land legs," she thought. "And I must get shoes."

The soles of her feet were red and peeling, toes burning. She'd never worn footwear, never been given any. In the past her greatest fear had been snakebite as she'd darted to the rice fields carrying messages from the massa to the slave driver. She had had to be quick to spy out that fast, evil coil in the grass. Now, although she refused to voice her complaints aloud, she needed shoes desperately, but for a very different reason. She was afraid her toes were going to freeze, maybe even drop off, and the last thing in the world she wanted was for her feet to look like Titan's. When the family finally reached their new house, she'd put on her new stockings. But not out in this wilderness, with no shoes to protect them. They'd be ruined in no time.

"Here," said Titan at last, dropping the bundles and taking off his hat to scratch his round, curly-haired head. He was standing next to a large pit about three feet deep. A couple of wooden boxes, a mat, a blanket, and some tools were spread untidily below him. A cracked china cup and jug sat on one of the boxes.

The three of them greeted one another thoroughly. Rachel told Titan of their new surname, and Mamma admired his hat.

Rachel nudged forward till her toes curled over the edge of the hole. To think Titan had been sleeping in this awful place. It was so small, like an animal's lair, and it reeked of earth, sea . . . and something worse. She sniffed. Mould, maybe. Bones. The smell reminded her of dead things, and she drew back quickly.

"Are you thinkin' of buryin' someone?" asked Mamma, staring into the pit wretchedly. "We can't live there. I ain't goin' to have my bebby there. I'm needin' a cradle for him, not a grave." She went quiet for a moment, then moaned, "Titan, where are your wits? You must've lost 'em when you crossed over the wide ocean." Sitting down on a large white rock, she fished a blanket out of her bundle, wrapped it around her, and began to sway back and forth.

Mamma was right. This hole was just like the one the Negroes dug at night back home to bury their dead in. Cleared of the boxes, it might hold two coffins, three in a pinch, certainly no more. Three. One for each of them. Rachel shuddered

at the thought, tried not to cry as the first stinging tears spiked through her lids.

"We got to build up the sides with wood,
maybe another two foot, sling a roof over. It'll do
us for winter, keep the snow out. In spring the
white bosses'll give us our land and we'll build a
proper house. Others roundabout are doing the
same thing."

This was a long speech for Titan, and he seemed
worn out with the effort of pushing it through his
teeth. But as he pointed away up the hill, Rachel
could see he was right. Dark wisps of smoke
spiralled up from what looked like holes in the
forest floor. People, perhaps other children, were
down underground, a whole village of them, living
in the dark. Well, if they could do it, so could she.

"How can I help, Titan?" she asked brightly,
swallowing the tears that had run down the back
of her nose into her throat. "I'm big and strong
as most grown-ups. I can fetch wood. I can hew
it if need be. Maybe we can get some kind of a
roof up before nightfall."

"Good for you," was his only reply. And for a fleeting moment he sounded like the white man on the ship who had written down their names.

"Seems a sad thing," Mamma remarked, "that you been here all this time buildin' houses for the white folk, but you ain't had time to build one for yoursel'." She got up and began to unpack the bundles, then bustled around starting to create a home for the three of them.

"That's the way of it, sure enough," said Titan. He slid into the hole to fetch his axe to cut wood with, and Rachel scrambled down too. It was only then that she noticed how he'd lined the earthen sides with ferns and pine branches to try to make things snugger for them.

Much, much later, while gathering moss to chink the spaces in the low wooden walls of their new hut, Rachel would suddenly remember Titan saying something about keeping the snow out. What was snow?

CHAPTER Nº 4

No one was talking in their dark home.
Titan hardly ever spoke anyway. There was little work to be had in the frigid weather, and he spent his time trying to fit his large body more comfortably into their small space. Mamma, dragging herself around and close to birthing the baby, had all but stopped talking too.

"Winter has frozen our tongues too cold to wag," she crabbed when Rachel remarked on how quiet it was. "And don' you go naggin' me, girl. Least you can stan' up in here. I got to walk around with legs or neck bent all the time, and Titan can't stan' up at all. This ain't the house I been wishin' for. This ain't the kinda life I been wishin' for, neither. Free Nigras, indeed."

It was bitterly cold, but Rachel was glad to get out, climbing through the trap door in the sloping roof and sliding down its icy surface to the ground before someone could call her back. She needed to be outside, to be free of her family for a while, even though the glacial weather would drive her back almost immediately. It was so cramped indoors, and any talk was a complaint.

But Mamma was right, she could see that. At least on the plantation they had always been warm, often too warm, with their bellies part full, even if only with yams or broken grains of rice. Here they were freezing every time they stepped out, half frozen when they stepped in, and their stomachs growled day and night like dogs howling at the door. And all they had by way of supplies was some cornmeal with white wriggly worms in it and a bit of what the

British called treacle. It was just molasses by another name.

"Not near enough to keep body and soul together," Mamma would grumble, as she cooked the cornmeal over the fire. "Only the worms are gettin' fat. How we s'posed to live out the winter like this?"

Rachel moved clear of the middens near the cabin and took a deep breath of frosty air. Ice and ashes, refreshing after the stink inside. Could it possibly be better to be a slave than a free girl? She was beginning to have worrying, disloyal thoughts.

Snow lay all over the rocky ground, had been there for days, so deep that it caught the weird imprint of her bare foot with its flattish heel and sole. She took another step and admired it, then skipped several times and did an untidy hand-spring. Her skirt flew up and breath streamed out of her in a white fog.

She'd known right away what snow was as soon as it had begun to drift down in fat, wet flakes. She relished its taste on her tongue and its tingle around her toes. The earth was softer to walk on, and she could draw pictures that stayed until there was a fresh fall. Now she made lacy patterns with her fingernail, took a stick and traced around her feet, then kneeled and wrote over and over the letters that she knew.

"That's an S, and that's a P," she said out loud, trying to spell "Sparrow" the way the captain had spelled it in his book. "I'll have to go inside soon. My feet are like blocks of ice. I can't feel them any more." She stopped for a moment to rub them. "That's a . . . oh dear, I recognize it, but I don't know what it's called. How am I going to learn to read if I don't even know my alphabet? And how am I ever going to be truly free if I can't read?" Rachel had heard another slave say that one time on the plantation, took it to mean that if you could read you could pull yourself up by your bootstraps if you had any, make a better life for yourself.

Something stirred behind a tree, and a faint, silvery spray cascaded through the branches.

"Who's there?" Rachel called. Her voice sounded strangely high in the snowy woods, where the air was so sharp and clear that nothing seemed quite real.

"Who's there, I say?" Was it an animal or a person?

A slight rustle was quickly followed by a flurry of movement. Rachel was almost sure she saw a long black braid fly out and slap across a trunk. It disappeared in a flash. Afterwards there was only silence and stillness. And a row of small, light footprints among the birches.

"It was a person," sighed Rachel, not sure whether to be pleased or scared. "A child, I think, a girl." There *were* children in Birchtown, other Negro children, but she saw them only rarely. Many were shoeless, like herself, and it was too wintry most of the time for them to venture out.

"But that wasn't a Nigra child," she decided suddenly.

When the words were out, singing in the cold air, she felt an awful wretchedness, a splash of

Rachel took a stick and traced around her feet, then kneeled and wrote over and over the letters that she knew.

loneliness. Whoever the child was, Rachel needed her company. But although longing to follow the prints till she found their owner, she realized it would be far too dangerous. Slowly, regretfully, she climbed up the roof to the trap door, slid inside, and dragged her stockings over her numb feet.

By Titan's reckoning, it was now Christmas, give or take a day. He said as much, surprising Mamma and Rachel with the sound of his voice. Then he set eightpence down on one of the boxes, his wages for a recent day's work. Everybody grinned, but a few minutes afterwards, Mamma put down the spoon she was stirring the supper with, leaned her arm against the wall, and groaned.

"Christmas, eh? Well, I think we're jus' about to get a present. Rachel, you better go fetch Nanna Jacklin, that ole bent lady with the scratchy voice. You know where she lives?"

"Yes, Mamma. By the shore, in the hut with three glass windows."

"Tell her to hurry. The bebby's comin', an' I need a woman with me."

Rachel was off and running. The forest was dense with snow, falling so thickly that she could barely see the outlines of trees. She moved rapidly from pine to pine, hugging each as she went, trying to keep her balance in the buffeting wind.

What was that? Her imagination must be playing tricks with her. A shadowy presence seemed to sway and shift, matching her progress step for step. She stopped, digging in her toes. It stopped. She started down the hill again.

Someone ran beside her.

Rachel's heart lunged into her throat. She turned and screamed, her voice hoarse with fear.

"Who's there? Tell me at once. You followed me the other day, too."

Nothing. The wind roared.

"Tell me. Show yourself now."

Still nothing.

"If you don't come over *here,*" shouted Rachel, trying to sound her bravest, "I'm going to come over *there* and fetch you. Just see if I don't."

There was a slight movement. At first she thought it was a bear, a huge winter bear, emerging from the veil of snow, and she almost died of fright. That would teach her to go yelling at strangers in the forest. But as it came closer she realized that this was a child of about her own age, an Indian girl cloaked in animal skins. The girl had long black hair which, unbraided today, blew out behind her, and she gripped something firmly in her slender hands.

"For you," she murmured in a gentle voice that nonetheless carried across the wind. She held out a pair of bright, soft shoes, high-ankled and beautifully beaded and quilled.

"Micmac moccasins," she whispered. "I wanted to give them before. I saw how cold you were, but I was too afraid."

Rachel slipped them on, stunned that anyone, never mind a perfect stranger, should give her anything. It was blissful, the way the fur lining comforted her frozen feet.

After admiring the shoes and their perfect fit for several moments, she remembered her manners and looked up to say thank you. The Indian girl had vanished.

Nanna Jacklin brought her grandson Corey with her to the Sparrow hut. A very little boy with filthy feet and hands, he was not above asking a bale of questions while his grandmother helped Mamma through her labour.

"Where you get them boots?" he asked Rachel.

"None of your business." He was far too young to be a playmate to her.

"Why your daddy got two toes missing?"

Titan was creeping around barefoot, trying to be useful.

"He's not my daddy, he's my stepdaddy."

"Where your real daddy, then?" Corey's hair looked as though no one had ever brushed it. It stood out in matted spikes around his head.

"He was sold away from the Roberts' place, where we lived." Rachel replied tersely. She moved as far away from Corey as she could in the cramped pit, but he came after her.

"Why he sold?"

"This is the last answer I'm ever going to give you. D'you understand?"

"Yessum."

"Well, then. Because he was a strong Nigra slave and someone offered the massa an armload of money for him."

"So why your *stepdaddy* got two toes missing?"

"That's it. I told you before. I've no answers left," snapped Rachel, much annoyed.

"Pleasum?"

"Oh, very well. But nothing else, never, ever. The massa cut them off after the first time he ran away. It slowed him up some, but it didn't stop him, else he couldn't have brought us here."

Titan heard and grinned. Then Mamma cried out and put an end to all the talk. Titan went over to her, holding her hand and pushing her hair back from the livid scar on her forehead.

"Bebby here," yelled Nanna Jacklin a few moments later. "A great big boy, jus' like his father, but he got all his toes! Fingers too, ten of 'em, ripplin' like corn in the field." She wrapped him in a bit of torn cloth and handed him to his mother.

"Where you get them shoes?" whispered Mamma hoarsely, heaving herself up on one shoulder.

"From an Indian girl, Mamma. She gave them to me."

"Well, you watch them Indians. They not our kind," she warned before sinking down again. "You need other Nigras to know where you are."

Rachel frowned and snuggled farther into her moccasins. Nanna Jacklin gathered her things and took Corey home.

The new baby had very pale skin, which made Rachel wince because it kept reminding her of the maggots in the cornmeal. But right away, everyone else loved the ugly creature, whose name was Jem. Mamma had decided beforehand she'd call a son that. A daughter, which was what Rachel had been hoping for, would have been Phebe.

"And you will be a bright gem, sure as the sun shines," Titan would say, enveloping the baby in his strong arms. "Maybe a hard diamond when you're grown."

Titan was so proud of his son that he'd taken to talking to him. As for Mamma, instead of her usual bossiness and complaints, there was laughter, and she crooned to the baby as she suckled him. At night she and Titan cuddled up with Jem between them, to keep the little mite warm. Rachel, who still couldn't understand what all the fuss was about, felt especially left out when no one even bothered to cook her a meal or admire her moccasins. She boiled her own cornmeal sullenly, spooning in more than her rightful share of treacle.

"Lookee here, Sukey. He's smiling at me," exclaimed Titan one day with great excitement as the baby displayed his little pink tongue and gums.

"Every grin gum don't mean smile," Mamma replied, smiling herself. "He mus' have the wind."

"Give him to me. I'll burp him." Rachel held her arms out. "I'm trying to love you, baby, I really am. But just look at you." She held Jem close to the fire so she could examine him properly. "Your skin is much too light, not Nigra skin at all, and your eyes are so blue I can see clear through them to midnight. They should be brown, boy."

"A bebby's jus' like cornbread not full-baked." Mamma had an explanation for everything.

"Well, he looks awful. And he sounds even worse," Rachel went on, as the baby began to squall. "Crying all the livelong day and driving me crazy."

"Hush, girl. You were jus' the same. You'll like him well enough when he's grown. He's gonna be a good frien' to you." Taking Jem, Mamma put him to her breast, closing her eyes as he sucked. She seemed to be shutting her daughter out completely.

"I don't need him. I already have a friend." Rachel muttered rebelliously. She was thinking of the Indian girl with the fly-away hair. She'd have to go out and find her. Anything to get away from that baby. They should put him in the rubbish.

CHAPTER N.º 6

She looked everywhere, but it seemed that the Indian girl didn't want to be found. Rachel watched for her footprints in vain, often with Corey trailing along. He seemed to have attached himself to her, and although she did her best to ignore him, he rarely fell back or stopped asking questions.

One morning Rachel went so far afield that she came upon a small town. She had a shawl on that she'd made from a bit of woven cloth, left over when Mamma tore up an old blanket to make wraps for Jem. Drawing it around her tightly, she peeked through the trees at the glint of brooding bay, with its dense cluster of wooden houses and banked-up snow.

"This must be Shelburne," she thought, remembering, with a small shudder, the scornful words of the crewman on the boat. Shelburne was a white town, not like the "Nigra stop" where Rachel lived.

Shelburne, as the man had hinted, looked nothing like Birchtown. The houses were bigger, for a start, some almost as big as the massa's house on the plantation. Many had barns and outhouses, and all but a few appeared to be brand new. In fact, most were so new they seemed barely finished, and others, scattered along long, straight streets, were still timber skeletons. Rachel guessed that they would be completed come spring. Maybe Titan would have a hand in the work and he could collect some more eightpences.

Despite the shin-deep snow, the place was thronged with people going about their business.

Most of them were white, but Rachel could see two Negroes, one shaking out a mat, the other pulling a heavy load along a snowy street. She felt encouraged to sneak down among them, almost as if their presence made her invisible.

She was still on the outskirts of the town, still among the tall pines, thinking how wonderful it must be to live there, with proper beds and fireplaces, with chimneys and front doors and stores nearby full (as she imagined) of food and fabrics, when a shrill, scathing voice cut in on her thoughts.

"Hey, Nigra. Whose Nigra are you?"

She turned abruptly, almost knocking over a tall, well-dressed white boy.

"I'm nobody's Nigra. I'm free," she said haughtily, drawing herself up to her full height and then adding an inch or two by standing on tiptoe. Pulling her shawl even more tightly around her shoulders, she scrunched down hard on her heels, wheeled around as fast as she could without falling, and began to move away as rapidly as possible.

But he darted by, and a second later he was standing in front of her again, tossing back his light brown hair.

"You'll go when I tell you to, and not before. I said, whose Nigra are you? Answer me properly this time."

Rachel had long understood that there were two ways of saying "Nigra." When Mamma and other Negroes said it, it was soft and open, like part of a lullaby. In some white men's mouths, though, it was harsh, painful, sounding like an insult. This boy, with his careless swagger and sharp, high voice, made it into the nastiest insult of all. He made it sound as though she were an animal.

"I told you, I'm free. I don't have a massa. My stepdaddy joined the British army and we were all released from slavery."

His eyes were ice blue. "Why, you stupid girl. You're one of those filthy urchins from Birchtown. How dare you come here and flaunt yourself among respectable white people?"

Rachel moved forward again, trying to get past him, but he stuck out his foot in its brass-buckled shoe and tripped her. She went sprawling.

"That'll teach you," he crowed. "I go to school and I know everything. You, on the other hand, you skinny great scarecrow of a Nigra, are ignorant as dirt. Now get out of here."

Rachel would have gone, would have been glad to. That's what she'd been taught all her life: to swallow the taunts and mockery of white people, even if, like now, she was burning with so much anger that she saw red splotches every time she blinked. But as she pushed her wrists down into the spiky crystals of snow to heave herself up and away, she spotted Corey hunched behind a tree. The little monster must have followed her all the way from Birchtown . . . without asking her a single question! No wonder she hadn't realized he was there.

Now, no matter what she'd been taught, no matter how dangerous it was to answer back, there was no way she was about to act the coward. Even if Corey was a little nobody who crouched shivering in the snow, he reminded her, very uncomfortably, of herself.

She scrambled up and glared directly into the tall boy's face. He might be as stuck up as a lord, he might think he knew everything, but there was one thing he didn't know: he had a thin stream of snot running from his nose to the dent in the middle of his upper lip. As it gathered there in a little pool, glistening and slimy as a snail track, somehow it changed everything. Why, under his fine clothes and his fancy shoes, she thought with a kind of frightened glee, he was just the same as everyone else.

"I'm not stupid and I'm not filthy," she said in a stately voice. "I may be poor but I'm as clever and good as you. Probably cleverer and better, in fact."

The boy was so shocked that for a scant second the wind went out of him, and his shoulders slumped. Rachel used that second to push her

Rachel tried to get past him, but he stuck out his foot in its brass-buckled shoe and tripped her. She went sprawling. Corey hunched behind a tree.

advantage. "And I mayn't go to school, but I can read and write anyhow," she said proudly.

"Nigras can't write," he blustered. "It's not allowed. None of our slaves can write."

So his family owned slaves. No wonder he behaved the way he did. And how sad that even in Nova Scotia there were still Negroes who had to obey a massa.

Rachel picked up a stick. The boy smashed it viciously out of her hand.

"I wasn't going to hit you, only show I can write," she remarked sadly. She knelt down in the snow and traced out R for Rachel with her index finger. Then she wrote S, P, A (she still didn't know what that letter was called, though she knew its sound), R, R, O, W. "That's my name," she said. "Rachel Sparrow."

"What a stupid name. This is mine," he said proudly. "Nathan A. Crowley." He picked up the stick he'd struck from her hand and wrote the letters in the snow. Now she knew how to say the A letter.

"What does the A stand for?" she asked.

"Archelaus," he said smugly. "After my grand-father."

He was now writing something else, a long something that was taking him such a deal of time that his tongue protruded with the effort and he panted his foggy breath into the air.

"What does that say?" she asked, trying desperately to commit the snow writing to memory.

"It says: 'Get out of here if you know what's good for you,'" sneered Nathan. "I knew you couldn't read."

"Oh, but I can now." She smiled. "Look." She repeated his words as she traced her finger under what he'd written. "You just taught me how. Thank you, Nathan Archelaus Crowley."

She dodged him and whirled away, laughing. Behind the tree, she could hear little Corey clapping.

Mamma was sick, coughing and moaning, tossing on the two boxes stuck together she called a bed. Titan was so worried that he went to fetch Nanna Jacklin.

"She's worn out with the bebby and the cold and the bad food. I ain't even got my herbs here in this God-forsaken place. I'm sorry, Titan, but there ain't nothin' I can give her." The old woman shook her head and went home.

Mamma wasn't even well enough to feed Jem. The baby cried listlessly until Rachel thought to dip a piece of cloth in treacle and give it to him to suck. But on the second night of Mamma's illness, he started to cough too, a harsh, brittle cough that sounded like dry twigs breaking. At dawn he was still hacking.

For a moment Rachel felt a tiny triumph. "Now you know what it's like to be hungry and miserable, like the rest of us," she thought. Then she felt ashamed, a deep, dark shame that sat in the pit of her belly and wouldn't shift. Jem was really sick, really starving, poor little helpless thing. It was all her fault, she knew it was, for wanting to throw him away.

She made up her mind. "I'm taking him outside, Titan. All the smoke and cinders in here can't be good for his chest."

"Cold air'll make him even sicker," said Titan.

"We have to do something. He'll die if we don't. He hasn't eaten for days, and now this."

Titan barely nodded before turning back to Mamma, who had broken out in a sweat and was trying to throw off her blanket. He was exhausted, Rachel could see that. He moved slow as a land-locked turtle to push Mamma's covers back over her. The whites of his eyes had turned yellow, and his eyelids sagged at the corners. Rachel felt sorry for him, sorry for them all, including herself. She was frightened, too, that Mamma might never recover. But she had to look after the baby. Mamma would expect her to.

After wrapping Jem in two scraps of blanket, she climbed through the trap door and slid outside with him. The sky was fine and clear, still blue-black down by the water, hazy pink through the pine trees to the east. She sat on a big flat rock and talked to him as he lay in the circle of her arms.

"I'm sorry, baby, I really am. I didn't mean for you to get sick. Now take a few breaths of this good air into your lungs and you'll feel a whole lot better."

Jem coughed.

"You must be feeling pretty bad. You haven't had any milk for a while. Now how would it be if I gave you something to take the edge off your thirst?"

Jem stared up at her with his strange, wise eyes, and Rachel suddenly felt he knew more than Mamma and Titan, more than Nathan Archelaus Crowley, more than anyone in the whole wide world. Perhaps he even knew how much she'd wanted him gone. Babies often looked that way, though. She'd noticed that with the missus' children. But by the time they were two, judging by the way they behaved, they'd forgotten everything.

She needed to try to love Jem, to think of him as a member of her family, no matter how hard it was. She bent forward and scooped up a few small speckles of fresh snow, rolled them together between thumb and forefinger, then thrust the miniature snowball she'd made into the baby's mouth. Jem sucked on it eagerly.

"Here's some more. It's just water, really, but it seems to be doing you a power of good."

She fed him till he wouldn't suck any longer, then sat quietly with him, watching the red sun thrust its way into the early sky.

"It's not that you've done anything wrong," she whispered at last. "Not really. It's just that you're taking my place with Mamma and Titan. I don't feel as if I belong any more. And they're all I've got. I don't have anyone else to belong *to*."

There was a flicker behind a tree. She wondered whether it might be Corey again, but she was suddenly too exhausted to go find out. Her eyelids were so heavy that she had trouble keeping them open. She began to drift, dream back her old landscape in Charlestown: grey moss dripping like dusty spiderwebs from a giant oak, intense heat, the song-like splash of the Cooper River.

She awoke with a start, half frozen. It was full daylight, and the Indian girl was sitting beside her. The girl had taken Jem into her own lap and was crooning to him in a strange soft language. The baby had his thumb in his mouth. His eyes were shut and he'd stopped coughing.

"Cold air is good for babies' coughs," the girl said gently. "It cleanses their lungs, makes their little bodies healthy again. My family have always known this. You did the right thing."

Rachel rubbed her eyes to make sure she wasn't dreaming. "My mamma is sick too," she confided to the girl. "I'm afraid she'll die. What can we do for her?"

"I'll fetch my aunt. If anyone will know what to do, she will. She's a healer."

Carefully, the girl handed Jem back to Rachel and, turning, sped off through the woods.

Many weeks later, Rachel took Jem outside again. Things were going well. The Indian girl's aunt had arrived right away with a great flourish, a good deal of harrumphing, and a skin bag full of Micmac medicine. She'd stayed till Mamma was on the mend, and now the two women, although still a little wary of each other, were almost friends. Rachel had even heard them laughing together.

Jem was thriving, and Titan was earning a whole shilling every day as a carpenter over in

Shelburne. That meant better meals and warmer clothing. Best of all, Rachel and the Indian girl, Ann-Marie, had become firm friends too.

Ann-Marie had shown Rachel how to chew up tiny bits of food and spit them into Jem's mouth so he wouldn't starve.

"Ugh! I feel like a mother bird feeding my baby a worm," said Rachel, dismayed. But Ann-Marie's trick worked. Jem grew strong, even though Mamma was too sick to nurse him. And as she took care of him, Rachel couldn't help but come to love him. She stroked his little head and sang to him. Sometimes she even thought of him as her baby.

Loving her brother was a precious gift, a gift that Ann-Marie had given her. What could she do for the Indian girl in return? All she had were words, with not too many stories to shape them into. Finally, she decided: she would tell Ann-Marie how they'd all run away from the plantation.

There had been many quilts in the massa's house. Every quilt, with its different pattern

Rachel decided she would tell Ann-Marie how they'd all run away from the plantation.

meant something important to the slaves. If Mamma was making the missus' bed and hung a certain quilt out of the window to air, it meant "stay away." Another quilt meant "massa fighting mad enough to whup someone." The day the Sparrows left, Mamma had hung out the most important quilt of all. It told Titan to come in from his work early. They were going to escape, run to the British army for protection.

This story led to another—how Mamma had got her scar. How the massa had been beating her when an edge of the lash had whipped round her face, almost taking out an eye. Mamma had vowed then, Rachel told Ann-Marie, that her family would be free some day.

"Lots of Nigras have scars like that, but Mamma was more shamed than most to be beaten. And it was for such a little thing. Taking a piece of bread from his table to give to her small hungry girl at home. That was me," Rachel said with surprise, as if she'd never fully realized it before. "She wanted to give the bread to me.

She told me once, but now she never speaks of it. It's a kind of hurting secret she carries with her."

"I'll never speak of it either," Ann-Marie promised, her dark eyes wide with shock.

For a while Rachel was scared that she had made a mistake in telling her friend. But she had nothing to worry about. In sharing Mamma's secret, the two girls became closer than ever.

Rachel was waiting for Ann-Marie now. She spread a blanket over a dry patch of earth and set Jem down on it. He stared up into the pines and waved his legs and arms in the air.

The trees smelled wonderful, fresh and faintly perfumed. They stole the stink of the pit cabin out of Rachel's nose. The snow was almost gone, slowly disappearing even from the dark places in the forest and the high places on the hills. There was a mildness to the air she hadn't experienced since coming to Birchtown.

"How you spell my name?" It was Corey, of course—Corey with his filthy feet, matted hair, and endless questions. He came whenever Nanna

Jacklin was gone about her business, and he still stuck to Rachel like a burr.

She moved to shoo him away, then changed her mind. She ought to be patient with him. It would be good practice for taking care of Jem as he got older.

"C, O, R—" She wrote the letters in the dirt by the blanket. "I'm not sure of the rest."

"Corey. That my daddy's name, too."

Rachel felt a stinging sorrow. A short time back she'd found out that Corey's daddy and mamma were both dead. They'd been caught escaping from their massa and shot. That's why Corey lived with Nanna Jacklin.

"Listen, Corey, I'm going to find out for you. Everybody should know how to spell their name. In fact, everybody should know how to read and write. I just have to figure how to get all that knowing out of Nathan Crowley's head and into mine. He's easy to fool, and I'll do it. Then I'll be able to teach you everything you need to become a smart, free man." She sat back, very pleased with herself. How difficult could it be?

Baby Jem smiled at her, a proper smile. Mamma had said he wasn't full-baked when he was born, but now he was browning nicely. And his eyes were starting to deepen to a lovely copper. Give him another month and he'd have proper Nigra eyes, just like Rachel's. He really did belong to their family. Mamma was right.

Rachel cooed at the baby. He cooed back.

Tufts of bright-green grass and yellow shoots were pushing out of the earth to gleam in the watery sun. A bird sang somewhere far off. Spring was coming, and Titan had promised them a new house come spring. She wondered idly if it would have glass windows, like Nanna Jacklin's and the rich people's houses in Shelburne. And whether there would be stores nearby, where she could buy herself a new shift and a proper petticoat.

"Why the snow melt?" nagged Corey, impossible as ever. He was digging in the hard earth with a pointed stick and looked dirtier than a chimney sweep.

"Because the weather's warmer, because the sun's out, because spring's coming, because winter's gone, because God is rewarding us, because, oh, I don't know." Rachel was laughing.

Jem, catching her eye, began to laugh too, a deep, throaty gurgle. As his mouth opened, she caught sight of two pearly buds—his first teeth! Whooping with joy, she jumped up, caught Corey by the hand so his stick went sailing into the air, and whirled him round till they were both giddy.

"Hello," called Ann-Marie, coming up the hill in time to watch them spin. "You are having a good time."

"Yes, we are," Rachel shouted. "That's because I've got spring in me today and I'm happy. I'm a free Nigra. A free Nigra in Nova Scotia. I'm going to learn to read and write whole sentences and I'm going to teach Corey how to spell his name."

"Good for you," Ann Marie replied, smiling.

Rachel went to fetch Jem. She lifted him high so that he could see the tops of the wide-branched apple trees close by the shore.

"This is going to be our home, baby," Rachel resolved. "Here at the Nigra stop in Birchtown. We live here, we'll always live here, and I don't want to see Charlestown, that horrid slave place, ever again. I'll make sure you never see it either."

And she meant what she said, every word of it.

Acknowledgements

Many thanks to my family and friends;
to Corey Guy, and to Clara and Earnestine of the
Jacklyn family, all descendants of the
original black Loyalists;
to Laird Niven, the archaeologist of the Birchtown site,
and to Patricia Clark of Seneca College, who were both
immensely helpful;
to Leona Trainer, my wonderful agent;
to Barbara Berson, my terrific editor;
to Cindy Kantor, who brought the idea for
the series to Penguin;

and

to Bookfriends, who are always an amazing source of
support and good humour.

MARIE-CLAIRE: BOOK ONE

DARK
SPRING

KATHY STINSON

MEET MARIE-CLAIRE

M ARIE-CLAIRE IS A FRENCH-CANADIAN GIRL LIVING in Montreal.

In 1885, when Marie-Claire is ten years old, Montreal is one of the filthiest cities in North America. Garbage is not collected regularly. Untreated sewage contaminates the river and even the streets. Smoke from the growing number of factories pollutes the air. The stench of it all, especially during warm weather, is downright disgusting.

The adults in Marie-Claire's life understand that filth is in some way partly responsible for people getting sick so often, but the building of water and sewage systems cannot keep up with the needs of the city's rapidly growing population.

Many people, attracted by business opportunities and jobs for unskilled workers, have been coming to Montreal from England, Scotland, Ireland, and from the

Quebec countryside. Anglophones tend to settle in the west end of the city, francophones in the east.

Living conditions are worst for people like Marie-Claire's family, the working class which makes up the majority of Montreal's population. They cannot afford the fine stone homes at the base of the mountain. That's where business owners, bankers, doctors, and lawyers live. Marie-Claire's family lives closer to the river, where homes made of wood are crowded closely together and have no indoor plumbing—conditions ideal for the spread of disease. Diphtheria, cholera, tuberculosis, and smallpox have all visited the city in recent years.

Religion is an important part of most people's lives, including children like Marie-Claire. This is reflected in the way the steeples of Montreal's many fine churches stand out prominently against the city's skyline.

Wages are low, however, and working conditions unsafe. Taking care of a home and family is hard work. Both parents, and sometimes children, work long hours, six days a week. If even one parent is unable to work for any reason, the family's survival will depend on the resourcefulness and resilience of almost every family member.

This is the Montreal in which Marie-Claire lives in the "dark spring" of 1885.

CHAPTER № 1

*Marie-Claire shivered in her thin night-*gown. The kindling in the wood stove snapped. When the flame began to lick at the larger pieces of wood, Marie-Claire replaced the iron lid on top of the stove. Wouldn't Maman be pleased to wake up with the fire already lit? She was still so tired after Philippe's birth. Marie-Claire did not know just what had happened in her parents' room that day almost a week ago, but she'd heard enough to know that having a baby must be harder work even than churning butter or hauling water.

Marie-Claire crossed the cold floor to where Emilie still slept, curled beneath the grey blanket. How tempting it was to crawl back into the warm bed with her sister until the heat of the wood stove took the chill from the air. But if she wanted everything to be ready before Maman awoke, she must keep moving.

She slipped on her boots and wrapped her shawl around her shoulders before crouching beside the bed and pulling from under it the chamber pot. She carried it carefully so its contents wouldn't slosh out before she got downstairs to the privy in the lane behind their house.

Already a set of footprints in the snow led to the door of the little wooden shed. Marie-Claire could hear her neighbour grunting inside.

"Hurry up, Monsieur Flaubert. It's cold out here."

The door swung open. "Mind your tongue, you sassy little girl."

Marie-Claire scowled. She wasn't a little girl. She was ten years old. Old enough to read and write and get up first and help Maman get the family ready for church.

She dumped her sister's nighttime urine down the hole, then lifted her nightgown and sat on the wooden seat, still warm from Monsieur Flaubert's big behind.

By the time Marie-Claire had emptied her parents' chamber pot, shaken the snow from her nightgown, hung it by the wood stove to dry, and got dressed, it was time to start breakfast. Marie-Claire put another stick of wood in the stove, poured water from the bucket into the kettle and set it on top. She cut five slices of bread from the loaf, ready to make toast—one piece for Emilie, one for Maman, two for Papa, and one for herself. Her baby brother was too little yet for more than the milk and water in his bottles, and her older brother had gone away with the army to help with a fight in the west. A fight with a man whose name—Louis—was the same as his own.

From the bedroom came a sudden cry. Papa appeared in the doorway holding Philippe awkwardly in his arms.

"Here, Marie-Claire, you take him. Maman is getting dressed and I have to pay a visit."

Marie-Claire crooned a song to the baby as she danced him around the room. *"D'où viens-tu, bergère? D'où viens-tu?"*

"Marie-Claire," Maman said, "did you light the fire this morning? Such a helpful girl you are becoming. And look at this bread, already sliced. It will have to be thin ones for the rest of the day, though."

"I am sorry, Maman. I was not thinking of later." This being Sunday, the market, of course, would be closed.

"Never mind, *ma petite*. Let me feed Philippe while you go wake your sleepy sister. We do not want to be late for church."

Marie-Claire crooned a song to the baby as she danced him around the room. "D'où viens-tu, bergère? D'où viens-tu?"

CHAPTER *N^o* 2

As they did every Sunday, as they had for as long as Marie-Claire could remember, her family met her cousin Lucille's family in the road and they walked together to the big church.

Except for the church bells, the streets were quiet that morning, the usual sounds of trotting horses, sleigh bells, and people calling to each other muffled by the heavy snow that had been falling all weekend. Wading through it, the women talked about the new baby and how little he slept between feedings. The men talked about how nice it was to sleep late this one day of the week when they did not have to go to work, although as a fireman Papa was sometimes called out no matter what day it was. As Emilie ran ahead with Lucille's little sister Bernadette, Marie-Claire and Lucille walked arm in arm, making plans for the future, when they would have big families of their own.

"Let's promise to live on the same street always," Lucille said.

Marie-Claire agreed. "That way we can do our laundry and take care of our children together, as my maman and yours do now."

Inside the church, the two families squeezed into their pews. The smell of wet wool and incense tickled Marie-Claire's nose in a pleasing way. The music from the organ sounded to Marie-Claire a little like crying, but it was a happy kind of crying, with her family—all except for Louis—kneeling together, elbows touching, thanking God for all their blessings. And Marie-Claire never tired of watching the hundreds of flickering candles while the priest preached the sermon and said prayers in his voice that was itself a little like music. "Please, God," he was saying, "accept today a special prayer for the well-being of our soldiers who have gone west to fight, and for an early end to the violence. Please, if it be part of your plan, bring these men home soon to their loving families."

"Oh, yes," Marie-Claire silently prayed, "please let Louis come home soon. Maman is worried about him, and Papa is worried too. I heard him say to my Oncle Henri that he does not like that Louis might have to fight against other French-speaking men. And I do miss him, dear Father, even if we do sometimes argue when he is helping me with my lessons."

Marie-Claire realized suddenly that everyone was standing. The organ was playing chords for the closing hymn. She rose quickly from her knees.

CHAPTER N°. 3

The snow continued to fall in fat flakes that clogged the streets. Going to school, Marie-Claire and Lucille carried their sisters on their backs, dumping them in huge drifts when they needed a rest.

The teacher, in her tidy black habit, a white wimple framing her stern face, scolded them in the doorway. "From the looks of your skirts, you have not been behaving as our Lord expects young ladies to behave."

"No, Sister," said Marie-Claire.

"We're sorry, Sister," said Lucille.

After school the girls thought nothing of how the Lord might expect them to behave. This was probably the last good snowfall of the season, and on the way home they ran and slid and jumped in the drifts. After checking that no adults were looking, Marie-Claire even threw a snowball at Jean-Paul, another of her cousins, who was on his way home from the boys' school.

"Let's build a snow fort," Lucille suggested.

In a great snowbank by the side of the road, Marie-Claire, Emilie, Lucille, and Bernadette dug and dug. Their fingers and toes were numb inside their thin gloves and boots, but in their dark little cave they giggled as they watched traffic go by, sleigh bells jingling from the horses' bellies as they pulled their carts and carriages through the heavy snow.

When one of the carts to go by was a fireman's hose wagon, Marie-Claire watched for the ladder wagon to follow. Where, she wondered, were the fire wagons going? Not to a house near where she lived, she hoped. So often, Papa had told her, when one house in a neighbourhood burned, so did others nearby.

But the ladder wagon did not come. Nor did a steam wagon. Perhaps the hose wagon was not on its way to a fire at all. It was odd that two firemen were riding in the wagon on top of the hoses.

A sudden unease gripped Marie-Claire. She crawled out of the snow fort into the street. The hose wagon was turning a corner—in the direction Marie-Claire lived. "Come, Emilie. We must go home. Hurry."

"Can't we play a little longer?"

"No. Come." Marie-Claire reached into the fort and yanked Emilie's sleeve.

"What is it?" Lucille said. "If you are worried your maman will be cross about your wet skirt, it is too late for that now."

"Something is wrong, Lucille. I know it."

Lucille and Bernadette ran to keep up with their cousins.

The fire wagon was parked in front of Marie-Claire's house, but the only smoke in the street came from chimneys. Marie-Claire ran up the stairs and, out of breath, pushed open the door.

The big shapes of two firemen filled the room. They were standing over Maman, who sat weeping in her chair. In Maman's hand a wooden spoon dripped gravy onto the floor.

Marie-Claire turned quickly to her sister. "You go with Lucille and Bernadette. I will come and get you later."

"What are those men doing here?" Emilie asked.

Marie-Claire pushed her sister out the door. "I will explain later."

In the cradle, Philippe was wailing. Marie-Claire picked him up to quiet him.

"Where is Papa?" She was afraid to ask, but had to know.

"Your papa is a brave man," one of the firemen said.

"I know that." Marie-Claire swallowed hard. "But I asked you, where is he?"

"It was a very bad fire," the other fireman said, "up in Saint-Jean Baptiste village. A burning rafter fell, your papa could not get out of the way in time."

"He is dead?" Marie-Claire ran to Maman's side. "You are telling me Papa is dead!?"

"No, no, not dead. No." The fireman crouched down. Marie-Claire looked into his soot-streaked face. The smell of smoke was heavy in his woollen uniform. "But he is badly hurt. He will be in bed for some time. Your maman will need your help to take care of him."

Marie-Claire cradled Philippe in one arm. "My papa, may I see him?"

"He is sleeping," Maman said. "Don't wake him."

Marie-Claire peered into her parents' bedroom. Papa's face was soot-black. His neck and one cheek were red, blistered, and shiny where someone had applied grease. One arm, tied to a board with white bandage, lay on top of his blanket. There were thick bandages around his shoulder, too.

How lucky they were, how lucky, that Papa had not been killed. Suddenly, in her wet clothes, Marie-Claire shivered. "Thank you, God," she whispered, "thank you. But please, if it is not too much trouble, while you are keeping Louis and the other soldiers safe out west, can you please help Papa to recover quickly?"

"Maman, what is all this?"

When Marie-Claire and Emilie came home from school, Maman was usually chopping cabbage or potatoes, stirring beans in the big pot on the stove, or going through the oats to take out mealworms before making porridge. Today, the wooden table was covered with piles of cut fabric. At a sewing machine, Maman was stitching two of them together.

"Shirts," Maman said. "At least they will be shirts when I have finished sewing them."

"So many?" Marie-Claire asked. Papa and Louis could not wear so many in a lifetime.

"Yes. Monsieur Grenier brings me the pieces that have been cut at the factory. He will bring more when these shirts are finished. Fortunately Tante Celine was able to lend me her sewing machine."

"You are working like poor Madame Masson up the road?"

"While Papa is unable to work. Yes." Maman's foot moved up and down on the pedal to keep the needle of the sewing machine moving as she spoke. "Will you get some onions from the pantry, please, and start chopping them?"

"How is Papa?" Marie-Claire found a corner of the table away from the shirt material and began to chop.

"Careful. Hold your fingers out straight. We don't want to find bits of them in the soup." Maman snipped the ends of thread from the seam she had just sewn. "Papa is in pain. It may be some weeks before he can get back to work.

While I am taking in sewing for Monsieur Grenier, I will need your help around here even more than before. I'm afraid you will have to miss school."

Marie-Claire hated the thought of missing school. The nuns were very strict, but Marie-Claire loved the arithmetic they were teaching—multiplying and dividing, much more complicated and fun than simple adding and subtracting.

Emilie tugged on the sleeve of Marie-Claire's dress. "Can you play with me?"

"Later, when I have finished making supper." But by the time Marie-Claire had finished chopping vegetables, fetched another bucket of water from the tap in the slushy back lane, set the soup on the stove, given Philippe a bottle, and taken Papa a mug of hot tea, it was time to help Maman clear the table of sewing. Supper was already late.

"Thank you, Lord, for the food you have provided," Maman said. "This is very good, Marie-Claire."

"Thank you."

"But a little more salt next time, eh?" With her fingers she took a pinch from the salt jug and sprinkled it in her bowl. "Tomorrow," Maman said, "we will need a bigger pot of soup. Your Tante Thérèse and Oncle Henri are coming."

"For supper?"

"Yes, and to live with us for a time."

"But where will they sleep?"

"Henri will sleep in Louis's bed. Thérèse will sleep with you and Emilie."

"Can't they just come for supper and then go back to their own house?"

"I cannot earn enough sewing shirts to make up for your papa's lost wages. Having your Tante Thérèse and Oncle Henri living with us will help us make ends meet. Also, as newlyweds, they are having trouble making rent payments. This will be a good arrangement for all of us."

"Maybe," Emilie suggested, "my Tante Thérèse can cook for us and take care of Philippe while you sew, so Marie-Claire can keep going to school."

"Thérèse cleans rooms at the hotel all day," Maman said, "while Henri works at the foundry. I'm sorry, Marie-Claire, if there was another way to manage . . ."

Some girls, Marie-Claire knew, were sent to live at the orphanage while their parents were having a difficult time. She would certainly rather give up school than do that. It was bad enough that Louis had to be away, but to be apart from her parents and from Emilie and Philippe, too? It was unthinkable.

Marie-Claire licked the last drip of soup from her spoon and brought the metal dishpan to the table. She lifted the square lid at the end of the wood stove.

"Oh, Maman. After I built up the fire, I forgot to fill the well with water."

"Don't worry," Maman said. "Let's just wash the dishes in cold water tonight. We're all tired." With grey circles under her eyes and her hair coming undone from its bun, Maman looked especially tired.

For a long time in the middle of the night, Maman was up with Philippe, trying to stop his crying. From her bed, Marie-Claire watched in the candlelight as Maman rocked him. She hoped he was all right. Their last baby, Pierre, had died when he was just a little older than Philippe. And the mess in Philippe's diapers lately was looking an awful lot like Pierre's did.

Marie-Claire slipped from beneath the blanket and knelt beside her bed for the second time that night. "Please, God," she whispered, "I love this baby so much. Please don't let Philippe die."

CHAPTER N° 5

The streets were slushy and muddy, and as Marie-Claire hurried along, she had to jump over many large puddles. Ice on the river groaned. People were saying that if it jammed this year at breakup, there would surely be flooding.

With every puddle she jumped, Marie-Claire recited another multiplication fact. "Six times three is eighteen." During her absence from school she did not want to forget all she had learned. "Seven times four is twenty-eight."

She called *"Bonjour"* to the organ grinder on the corner but could not stop today to talk. She had to fetch, before the store closed, more of the medicine that would stop Papa from crying out in his sleep. He got out of bed in the daytime now and did his best to be cheerful, but Marie-Claire could see in the tight muscles of his face that it took great effort.

In the square, not far from where she would buy the medicine, huge but shrinking lumps of ice were all that remained of the wonderful ice palace that had stood there during the winter carnival. What a sight it had been—the glassy walls glistening in the sun like giant diamonds, flags of France and England flapping snappily in the cold wind. Many times Marie-Claire and Lucille had admired the palace till their toes grew numb.

"Imagine being a servant in such a castle," Lucille had said.

"If you are going to imagine," Marie-Claire had answered, "why not imagine being the Snow Queen?"

How long ago that seemed now. How much easier life had been then—before Louis went away, before Papa's accident, before Maman started sewing for Monsieur Grenier and Philippe was still safe inside her, when there was time for going to school and playing with Emilie and Lucille. Except for church on Sundays and the times Lucille came around with Tante Celine when she brought extra bread or soup, the girls had hardly seen each other at all since Papa's accident.

With the bottle of medicine now in her pocket, Marie-Claire longed to get on the streetcar, to sit on one of the wooden benches in the covered cart and let the horses pull her tired body closer to her home. But even with the wages of her aunt and uncle coming into the house, there were no extra nickels for streetcar fare. She would just have to pick her way as best she could around the garbage appearing in disgusting piles with the melting of the snow.

"It's terrible," her Tante Thérèse was saying when Marie-Claire entered the house, shaking mud from her skirt. "Just terrible. Their arms were swollen hard like big red balloons. And the fevers! You can't tell me this is better than smallpox."

"Whose arms?" Marie-Claire asked. "What fevers?"

"Marie-Claire, you're interrupting," Maman said, re-threading the needle on the sewing machine.

"It's all right, Hélène. At the orphanage—I heard about this at the hotel today, one of the cleaners there does some work for the nuns, too—at the orphanage, doctors came to give the children a needle. They say it's to keep them from getting *la picotte,* but you should see them. It's terrible. Me, I'd rather be sick than go through what those poor children . . ." Thérèse shook her head. "Apparently, a few people in the city are sick with smallpox and the doctors say it could spread. Sure it's bad, those ugly spots you get, but what's a few people? Do we know anyone who has it? No. What I know is, those needles they want to give are horrible."

"Will I have to get a needle, Maman?"

"Of course not. Be a dear now and see if Papa wants some of his medicine."

Huge slabs of ice cracked and heaved along the banks of the river. Warm winds rippled the surface of puddles, growing larger by the hour, in the streets and back lanes.

From his chair at the end of the table, where he was now able to sit comfortably for some hours, Papa said, "The noise of that river breaking up reminds me of artillery fire."

Marie-Claire placed a bowl of beans in front of him. "When I was down there yesterday, I could hear the river humming. *Humming,* Papa, like it is something alive."

"It speaks, it moves, it rises and falls—who knows, maybe it *is* alive."

When the river flooded, its waters flowed over the harbour wall. They flowed on through the lower streets of the city where Marie-Claire and her family lived. The river water mixed with the filthy water draining down from the mountain. Water continued to rise till it covered sidewalks and seeped under doors.

Looking out the window, Papa said, "The family downstairs will be in it up to their ankles. We must invite them to come up here until the flooding recedes."

Marie-Claire's already crowded home became even more crowded as the grateful Flauberts dripped in carrying blankets and food. Monsieur Flaubert brought his fiddle, too. After supper that night the families sang and laughed together until Papa said, "I must get to bed."

Above the sound of Monsieur Flaubert's snoring, Marie-Claire heard Papa cry out sharply in his sleep, then Maman lighting a candle and rustling around for his medicine. "I am getting better," Papa whispered. "It is only at night . . ." Beside Marie-Claire her Tante Thérèse rolled over and mumbled something in her sleep. Emilie's hand reached up and stroked Marie-Claire's cheek.

On the floor, Monsieur Flaubert stopped snoring. His little boy said, "Is it morning yet?"

"Not yet, *chéri,*" Madame Flaubert whispered. "Go back to sleep."

Marie-Claire closed her eyes. "Thank you, God, for keeping us all safe here, but please can you stop the flood by morning? Our house is really not big enough for all these extra people."

Outside, something thumped against the house. A chunk of wood maybe? Another dead cow? Was the spring flooding worse this year than last? Was God angry at the people of Montreal for something they had done or not done?

The next day, Marie-Claire hauled in extra buckets of water and boiled Philippe's diapers without complaining. She kept Emilie and the Flauberts' little boy entertained with stories. Muddy water continued to lap against the sides of the house. Except to visit the privy and the community tap, awash in flood water, no one ventured out.

By lunchtime they had eaten all the bread. Tante Thérèse suggested that she and Madame Flaubert could make some biscuits. Maman said, "Don't use any milk in them, please. Philippe will need what we have for his next bottle. The last one I gave him was mostly water."

Marie-Claire opened the window and leaned out. Could she see, above the muddy water, a wet line on the walls of the houses across the street?

How much farther did the water have to fall before they could go out? She was about to close the window when, standing on some kind of raft, her cousin Jean-Paul appeared.

"Marie-Claire," he shouted, "is there anything I can bring your family?"

"Where did you get your raft?"

"The sidewalk on my street is busting up. I tied a couple of boards together, and *voilà!* Using another board for a paddle, I can go anywhere."

"Can you bring us some milk, Jean-Paul, for the baby?" She tossed down an earthenware bottle with some money in the bottom, which Jean-Paul caught neatly.

In twenty minutes he returned and tossed the bottle back up to the window. "Good catch, Marie-Claire," he said.

CHAPTER N° 7

Finally, several days later, the Flaubert family returned home.

"Maman, I wish my Tante Thérèse and Oncle Henri would go home too." They were both out at work, so Marie-Claire could speak freely as she scraped the scales from the fish she was preparing for supper.

"We are lucky to have them here." Maman guided two pieces of material under the up-and-down needle of the sewing machine. "Without their help, I don't know what we would do while Papa is unable to work."

"I could go to work at the tobacco factory," Marie-Claire suggested. "Josephine has a job there."

"Anyone who would hire such a young girl I do not want you working for. Besides, if you went away to work, who would help me here?"

"I can help you, Maman," Emilie said, rocking Philippe's cradle in the corner.

Maman was right, of course. Emilie could clean boots and help a little with the baby, but she could not do the work that was now Marie-Claire's—shopping, preparing meals for the family, hauling water for cooking, and cleaning and laundry. So many diapers she boiled every day. Also, even if she could take a paying job, as a child her wage would be very small.

"Maybe if I help you more," Marie-Claire said as she dumped fish guts into the slop bucket, "you can make even more shirts, and we won't need my Oncle Henri and Tante Thérèse any more."

Maman stopped the whirring machine. "Why do you want them to leave, Marie-Claire? I thought you liked them."

"I do. But beside me in bed my Tante Thérèse does not always smell very nice. And why does my Oncle Henri have to shout all the time? I am sure the Flauberts downstairs can hear every word he says."

"I'm afraid," Maman said, "that your Oncle Henri is losing his hearing. He does not realize he speaks so loudly."

"Losing his hearing? He is not much older than Louis, is he?"

"All the clanging and banging of machinery at the foundry twelve hours a day, six days a week—it is a wonder Henri can hear at all after two years working there."

Marie-Claire nodded. But still, she longed to have things at home back as they should be.

Before going to the market the next day, Marie-Claire slipped into the church to sit by herself in the quiet and remember what it had been like before the burning rafter crashed down on Papa. Sunlight shone in through the stained-glass windows.

"Please, God, help me be more patient with our crowded house, and don't let my Oncle Henri get any more deaf than he already is. Please can you try to mend Papa's shoulder a little faster? And please don't let my dear Lucille forget we are friends at this time when I cannot go to school or play with her." Afraid that asking so much would make her appear ungrateful, Marie-Claire added, "Thank you for keeping Philippe alive, even if he is still so sick, and thank you for getting Maman to say I don't have to get the awful needle that did bad things to the arms of the children at the orphanage."

On Sunday, with the candles flickering and the organ playing its sad but everything-will-be-all-right music, Marie-Claire bowed her head and said the same prayer. During the sermon, she leaned slightly forward and glanced along the pew to where Lucille sat, with her back straight and her hands folded in her lap. Lucille must have felt her friend's eyes upon her because she turned then toward Marie-Claire and smiled warmly.

"Let us pray," the priest said. He prayed that members of the congregation should choose the correct path, be grateful for their blessings, and honour God in their daily words and deeds. He prayed that the troops from Montreal should not be sent into the thick of the fighting in the west.

Marie-Claire was shocked to realize she had forgotten her big brother in her personal prayers. "Dear God," she quickly prayed, "forgive me for being selfish, please, and keep our Louis safe."

CHAPTER N.º 8

Day by day, as summer approached, the smell in the streets got worse. Barrels of manure overflowed into big puddles in laneways. Dead rats sprawled among rotting heaps of vegetable scraps, fish, eggs, and bones. One morning, between her home and the market, Marie-Claire counted six of them—and two dead pigs so disgustingly decayed that they must have been drowned in the floods earlier in the spring.

Around the market, where there were no privies at all, and where sewer drains were clogged with everything the butchers and other stall-keepers tossed out, Marie-Claire twice had to grasp her stomach and will its contents not to come up. With every step she took, something squished underfoot.

As she did the shopping, Marie-Claire did her best to remember all that Maman had taught her. Don't let anyone sell you meat that has maggots in it. The apple woman with the scar on her cheek has the nicest apples. Watch that the man selling flour does not put his finger on the scale. Don't ever pay for anything the first price you are given.

Marie-Claire roamed among barrels and baskets and carts, jostling against the other girls and women out to shop and catch up on the latest news and gossip.

"I hear the city hired a new scavenging company, cheaper than the old one, but are they doing *anything* to clean the streets?"

"He's bringing little enough money into that house and then he drinks most of it away."

"Can't you just smell the disease in all this filth? No wonder we've got smallpox in this city."

"But what would you have her do, Claudette?"

"Oh, I heard it is all over. A few cases there were, that is all."

"I hope so. A dreadful illness it is. If it doesn't kill you, its spots can leave you scarred for life."

"If you do get it, don't let the black wagon take you. In hospital you are almost sure to die."

With a cabbage, some carrots, and a few potatoes in her basket, Marie-Claire headed to a stall where chickens hung by their feet.

"How much for that one?" she asked. When the vendor reached up, she said, "I'm here to buy meat, not skin and bones. I was asking about the next one over."

The vendor placed the chicken on his scale. "Forty-five cents."

Marie-Claire wished she had enough money in her pocket to just pay it. She hated arguing for a better price. But Maman had said, "They don't expect you to pay what they ask." And it wasn't really arguing, it was bargaining.

Marie-Claire took a deep breath. "Not worth it," she said, and as Maman had taught her, she began to walk away. She hoped the next farmer would not be charging even more for his chickens.

"All right then, forty-one cents. Six cents off."

Marie-Claire turned back. "Six cents off makes thirty-nine." Holding herself tall, her heart pounding in her chest, she said, "I will pay you thirty-six."

The vendor handed Marie-Claire the chicken. "I am going to be a poor man at this rate."

"*Merci, monsieur,* thank you."

The man laughed as she headed off to buy a loaf of bread and a bag of beans.

With a few cents left in her pocket, Marie-Claire went to a stall inside the long marketplace and bought some beef bones. Sometimes a little broth in Philippe's bottle helped him sleep a little longer before waking again with his awful little cry.

Philippe stopped making the foul messes in his diaper. It seemed he was getting better. But one morning, after emptying the chamber pots, Marie-Claire realized that the house was oddly quiet. She ran to her parents' bedroom.

"I am sorry," Maman said. "Philippe passed away in the night. He was not strong enough."

"Why, Maman? Why wasn't he strong enough?" Tears streamed down Marie-Claire's cheeks.

Maman stared into the cradle. "It is God's way."

"But two babies in one family? It is not fair!"

Maman's lips almost disappeared in a thin line. "It is God's way."

Marie-Claire's bones felt heavy, but she tried to work fast that day so she could go to meet Lucille when she came out of school. She had to talk to someone who would understand how sad she felt. Maman seemed to have no heart left in her at all.

"But your maman is right," Lucille said. "It is not ours to question why God chooses those he does. And there are many babies God lets us keep for just a short while."

"That is all very easy for you to say. You have not had two babies die at your house before they had even one birthday."

"It is a shame your maman must spend so many hours sewing . . ."

"Are you saying it is Maman's *fault* that Philippe died? Or *mine*?! Lucille, you horrid witch! How can you be so cruel? You are as cruel as . . . as God!"

Marie-Claire hurried so she could meet Lucille after school. She had to talk to someone who would understand how sad she felt.

"Marie-Claire! You will be punished for saying such a thing. You had better hurry now to church and beg forgiveness."

"I will not! And I will never speak to you again! I wish instead of Philippe it was *you* who was dead!"

CHAPTER N.º 10

Throngs of people packed the streets singing hymns. No one wanted to miss the parade for La Fête Dieu, winding its way, under golden banners and a hot sun, to Notre Dame. As crowds flocked into the vast church with twin towers, people agreed that this had been the grandest procession yet.

For Marie-Claire it was not. It was the only spring celebration of earthly blessings she had ever attended without Lucille.

In spite of the warm stuffiness of the church,

Emilie leaned against Marie-Claire in the crowded pew. Marie-Claire wrapped an arm around her little sister.

"Are you sad too?" she asked.

Emilie nodded. "Philippe never got to see a festival," she whispered.

"I know." If only Lucille understood.

All around, people's heads were bowed in prayer. Marie-Claire bowed her head too, but once again, like every day since Philippe's death, prayers would not come.

Coming out of the church, Marie-Claire and Lucille avoided each other's eyes, but Marie-Claire noticed how flushed her cousin's face was. Had it been that hot inside, or was Lucille ashamed of the cruel things she had said? Good. She should be. Or maybe she had a bad fever. That would be fine too.

Marie-Claire took Emilie's hand and Maman's arm and, without a word to Lucille, stepped into the street. Such mean thoughts she could not stop herself thinking. Perhaps she was herself a bad person—fighting with her best friend, being glad if she had a fever. Being unable to think of something to thank God for was bad too, and the feeling she had that asking him for anything was pointless, because hadn't he let Philippe die, and wasn't Louis still out west, and wasn't Papa still unable to go back to work at the fire station?

Back home Emilie played quietly with her clothespin doll. Papa and Oncle Henri smoked their pipes while Tante Thérèse plucked a chicken and Maman chopped carrots. Maman never did her sewing on Sundays.

The pieces of fabric waiting to be sewn on Monday sat piled in the corner. Some of the pieces were quite small. About the right size, Marie-Claire thought, for a little dress for Emilie's naked doll.

Not wanting to interrupt the conversation Maman and her Tante Thérèse were having, she took one of the smallest pieces of fabric from the pile, threaded a needle and, wrapping the material around the neck of Emilie's doll, sewed her a

*Marie-Claire took one of
the smallest pieces of fabric
from the pile and sewed
a dress for Emilie's doll.*

dress. It was just a simple little dress, gathered around the neck and stitched down the back, but Emilie beamed.

Marie-Claire smiled. Maybe she wasn't such a bad person after all.

CHAPTER N⁰ 11

The bishop was dead. Gathered round the table the day after La Fête Dieu, Marie-Claire's parents could talk of nothing else.

"We have so much because of him. Schools and hospitals, organizations to help the poor."

"Not to mention all the new churches."

"So beautiful . . ."

"He was a good man."

"A fine bishop."

But is death such a sad thing, Marie-Claire wondered, when someone is so old? There had been less talk about little Philippe, yet how much more her heart ached at his passing.

So much was the bishop loved that the procession for his funeral was even bigger than the parade for La Fête Dieu. Marie-Claire could hardly believe the hundreds of carriages and thousands of people in the streets. Among the faces were several, she noticed, covered in spots. Could these people have the smallpox her aunt and women in the market had spoken of? Were there now more than just a few cases of it in the city? Marie-Claire had only a moment to wonder before she was caught up again in the spectacle of bands, horses and carriages, bishops, police, students, nuns, and important men, all clutching prayer books or rosaries as they marched by.

Never before, Marie-Claire was sure, could the church have been so packed. Even when all the pews were filled, people continued to pour in the doors. From every pillar hung black-and-orange banners, like those hanging on many of the buildings outside.

Marie-Claire snuggled in close to Papa. It was wonderful to have him back at church. He had been exercising his arm and shoulder a lot and was able to sit and even stand for long periods now without having to go and lie down.

"A person would have to be dead himself," Papa said, "not to attend the funeral for such a great bishop as Ignace Bourget."

The chanting of the choir of hundreds echoed throughout the vast cathedral and hummed right through Marie-Claire's body. It put something back inside her, somehow, that had been missing. She bowed her head and thanked God at length for his many blessings, even for letting them have Philippe for a while. She thanked God for giving her back her ability to pray.

When she finished praying, she looked around for Lucille. She must be here today. Where was she? Marie-Claire wanted to go to her and tell her she forgave her the awful things she'd said and apologize for her own hurtful words. She found Lucille a few rows behind, between her

When Lucille looked up, Marie-Claire's heart dropped into her stomach. Angry red spots covered Lucille's face. It had to be smallpox.

parents, her head bowed. She would speak to her when the service was over.

When Lucille looked up, Marie-Claire's heart dropped into her stomach. Angry red spots covered Lucille's face. Some of the spots oozed shiny pus.

Smallpox? It must be. But had her Tante Thérèse or someone not said that people could die of this ugly thing? *Lucille, I wish you were dead.* That was what she, Marie-Claire, had said.

"Oh, dear God, please, no!"

CHAPTER N° 12

"*Marie-Claire, what is this?*" Maman's voice cut like an axe into Marie-Claire's absent-minded stirring of the soup. "Did you do this?"

Maman held up Emilie's little doll, still proudly wearing the dress Marie-Claire had made. Maman's face was pulled into an angry scowl, angrier than Marie-Claire had ever before seen.

"I did, Maman. Emilie was so sad, I wanted to do something to make her feel a little better."

"And so you took something of mine without asking?"

"You were busy. It was just a little piece. I—"

"A whole shirt ruined because of *just a little piece*. You foolish, foolish child! Do you think Monsieur Grenier will pay me for a shirt that is missing a cuff?" Maman shouted. "No! He will charge me a fine for the ruined shirt! And after all the work I have done!"

"I am sorry, Maman, I truly am. I didn't know."

"As if things were not difficult enough!"

"I know, I know, I said I am sorry! What else can I do?!" Without waiting for an answer Marie-Claire ran from the house.

It wasn't fair. All she took was one little cuff! Was it her fault Maman worked for such a mean boss? Was that any reason to be so mean herself? It wasn't fair at all, when Marie-Claire worked so hard to cook, clean, take care of Emilie, do shopping and laundry, while all Maman did was sit around sewing shirts.

A hot, damp breeze blew off the river.

Of course, that wasn't true. Maman worked hard too. Marie-Claire had often seen her wince as she tried to stretch her back after so many hours bent over the sewing machine. And now, because of her awful daughter, Maman would not get all the money she had earned.

Everything, it seemed, was because of her, Marie-Claire. Maman being upset, and the family being short of money. The fact that her cousin Lucille was sick and dying was her fault too. Marie-Claire ran and ran, but she could not get away from herself.

At the market, with a stitch in her side and sweat pouring down her forehead, she trudged aimlessly from stall to stall. Tonight before bed she would pray for a good long time. She would ask God to help her be a better person. In the meantime—yes, she had a little change in her pocket left over from the trip to market when she had got such a good bargain on a block of cheese. Was it enough to buy a loaf of the bread Maman especially liked but bought only for special occasions? It would not make up for the ruined shirt, and maybe Maman would be angry if she spent money on bread unnecessarily, but Marie-Claire wanted so much to make some kind of peace offering.

Luck was with her. The bread was a day old and she got it at a very good price. Quickly she made her way toward home, her dress sticking to her back.

"Marie-Claire! Come!" Jean-Paul shouted. "On your street! The black wagon!"

Marie-Claire hugged the loaf of bread she had bought and ran behind Jean-Paul to the end of the dirt lane where she lived. Outside Lucille's house was parked the black wagon. Policemen were shouting at Lucille's father.

"She must go!"

"No. Please!" Lucille's father begged. "We can take good care of her at home." Behind him cowered Lucille, tears streaming down her spotty face.

Marie-Claire had heard that people with *la picotte* were sometimes forced to go in the black wagon to the hospital, but her best friend? "This is not possible," she whispered. She must go to Lucille right now and beg her forgiveness. She must pray to God to correct this awful mistake.

But before she could get near Lucille, the doors of the black wagon, with Lucille inside, slammed shut.

CHAPTER N.º 13

Throughout all the singing and speeches on Saint-Jean Baptiste Day celebrating the survival of the French-Canadian people, Marie-Claire could think of and hope for the survival of just one of them. "Lucille, Lucille, you must get well."

So that her Tante Celine could go and visit at the hospital, Marie-Claire offered to take care of Lucille's little sister. She took Bernadette and Emilie down to the river to watch the men in shirt sleeves loading big sacks, barrels, and boxes onto the huge ships.

When the girls tired of that, Marie-Claire tied a rope to a lamppost and turned it and turned it till finally the girls grew tired of skipping, too. At home, she worked fast and hard as if, if she could just be good enough, it would help ensure Lucille's recovery. "And please, God," she prayed, "can you try to prevent the spots from leaving permanent scars? Lucille has such a pretty face."

When, two weeks later, Marie-Claire heard that Lucille was home, she whooped with joy.

"Please, Maman, may I go and see her?"

"Of course. Go. You have been working your fingers to the bone here. You'll be an old woman before you're twelve years old at the rate you've been going. Go now. I'm sure Lucille will be pleased to see you."

Will she? As Marie-Claire passed the scavengers shovelling slimy garbage into wagons, she wondered.

"Come in, Marie-Claire, come in." Her Tante Celine was up to her elbows in flour. "Lucille is just picking over the oatmeal for me. It's so good to have her home again."

Lucille's head was bent over a sack on a chair in front of her. With her fingers she gently sifted the oats, pausing occasionally to toss a mealworm into the fire.

As if sensing something between the girls, Tante Celine suddenly wiped her hands on her apron, said, "I just remembered something I must be doing," and left them alone.

"Lucille, I came to apologize," Marie-Claire said quickly. "I am sorry for what I said." When Lucille said nothing, Marie-Claire went on. "I cannot stand it when we argue. I said things I did not mean and I was so afraid—oh, Lucille, you don't know how afraid I have been. When you went to hospital I thought you would die and it would be all my fault."

"Do you really think you are as powerful as all that?" Lucille looked up at Marie-Claire for the first time. Faded spots still marked her forehead and one cheek. "And do you honestly think you were more frightened than I?"

"No. Of course not. No. But please, Lucille . . ." Marie-Claire pulled a chair over beside her cousin and sat down. "Can you please try to find it in your heart to forgive me?"

"Marie-Claire, can you imagine being in hospital, your throat parched and your ugly skin burning up and no one comes for hours with a glass of water or a cool cloth? Can you imagine lying there and beside you in the next bed a girl has died and you call for the nuns to come, but there are so many patients, who knows when they will?"

Marie-Claire let her tears drop into her lap. After all Lucille had been through, it was no wonder she could not forgive her.

"But it is not your fault I got smallpox," Lucille continued. "It is not your fault I went to hospital. There are so many people in the city with the disease now, they are saying it is an epidemic. And of course . . ." Lucille smiled then, "of course I *must* forgive you. I could not bear it either when we were not speaking."

Marie-Claire pushed the oatmeal bag out of the way, threw her arms around her cousin, and kissed her on both cheeks. Her face must have betrayed what suddenly occurred to her, because Lucille laughed and said, "Don't worry. They would not have sent me home if I were still contagious."

"To be honest, Lucille, I would be more worried if we could not be friends again than I ever could be about getting sick."

"We *are* friends again." Lucille grabbed Marie-Claire's hands and squeezed. "We are friends now, and we will be friends forever."

CHAPTER 14

Papa stood in the middle of the room wearing only an undershirt and trousers. In each hand he held an iron pot. With his arms stretched to either side, he slowly lifted the pots up and over his head. Slowly he lowered them again to his sides.

"Josèph, it is wonderful how well you are getting back your strength," Maman said, "but isn't that enough for today?"

"Nonsense," Papa said. "Put some potatoes in these pots so I can work these muscles harder."

"I'll work those muscles for you," Oncle Henri suggested, rolling up his sleeves. "Come on, Josèph. How about it?"

Papa set down the pots and faced Oncle Henri across the table. "Ready?"

Elbows braced on the table, the men locked hands.

"Go."

Each man tried to push the other's hand down flat to the table. Blood vessels stood out on the backs of their clenched fists. Raised knots of muscles in their arms and across their shoulders quivered. Marie-Claire clenched her own fists, as if doing so would add to Papa's strength.

After a long minute, sweat shone on Papa's face, his arm began to tremble, and Oncle Henri was able to push Papa's hand a little closer to the table. Grunting, Papa pushed back. When the two clenched hands were again upright, Marie-Claire and Emilie cheered. Oncle Henri eventually got Papa's arm down to the table, but still the girls cheered. So much stronger Papa was getting.

In time he was strong enough to carry hoses, buckets of water, even another man if necessary. The day he returned to work, Marie-Claire put extra chunks of ham in his beans and packed an extra-thick slice of bread and butter in his lunch box.

When Monsieur Grenier came to pick up Mama's shirts and bring her more pieces to sew, Mama said, "Bring me only half this number next week. My husband is back at work now. And I must get back to my work here at home so my daughter can get back to school."

At the end of the room, where she was scrubbing the floor, Marie-Claire smiled.

That night, after the family had given thanks for the food they were about to eat, Oncle Henri announced in his big voice, "Thérèse and I will soon be leaving you."

"Why?" Maman asked.

"Where will you go?"

"You don't need us here any more," Thérèse said, "and I heard at the hotel that the men we sent out west are on their way home. Riel has fled, and the rebellion is over."

Marie-Claire dropped her fork to her plate. "Our Louis is coming home?"

"If it be God's will," Maman said, her voice full of hope.

"Oh, please, God, let it be so," Marie-Claire exclaimed. "But, my Tante Thérèse, do you and my Oncle Henri have to go? We can make room here for everyone."

Maman smiled, then looked to Thérèse and Henri. "Perhaps your aunt and uncle have other reasons to be finding a home of their own?"

"We are going to go to Toronto," Oncle Henri said. "I hear they pay men a decent wage there."

"But, Henri, you will not find many French people in Toronto," Papa said.

"My English is pretty good," Henri said. "We will be all right."

The festive mood at the table seemed broken by this news. Everyone was chewing quietly when Tante Thérèse spoke again. "Also, when winter comes, our household will have an additional little member."

"We are getting a dog?" Oncle Henri teased. "You didn't tell me!"

Tante Thérèse laughed. "If Henri finds a good enough job, we will all be able to come on the train to visit you here at Christmas."

Such a long time away Christmas seemed now, with the suffocating heat of summer wrapped tight round them.

"Let us give thanks," Papa said, "for your good fortune."

"And for the hope that Louis may be home soon," Marie-Claire added.

"And for Josèph's recovery," said Maman.

"For all the good things in life," Oncle Henri shouted, "let us say *merci infiniment!*"

Together everyone at the table said, "Amen."

ACKNOWLEDGEMENTS

I WOULD LIKE TO THANK THE FOLLOWING FOR THE PARTS THEY PLAYED IN THE DEVELOPMENT OF THIS PROJECT: MY AGENT, LEONA TRAINER, FOR HER CONFIDENCE IN ME, FOR BRINGING TO ME THE OPPORTUNITY TO CONTRIBUTE TO THE OUR CANADIAN GIRL SERIES, AND FOR HER SUPPORTIVE INPUT; MY PARTNER, PETER CARVER, FOR HIS SUPPORT ALSO AND FOR HIS PATIENCE DURING THE PERIOD WHEN I SEEMED TO THINK OF LITTLE BUT MONTREAL HISTORY, SMALLPOX, AND MARIE-CLAIRE'S LIFE; MY EDITOR, BARBARA BERSON, FOR DEVELOPING THE SERIES AND DOING WITH *DARK SPRING* WHAT GOOD EDITORS DO; CINDY KANTOR, WHO BROUGHT THE IDEA FOR THE SERIES TO PENGUIN; BARBARA GREENWOOD, GILLIAN O'REILLY, BILL FREEMAN, AND MARIA VARVARIKOS FOR SUGGESTING POSSIBLE RESOURCES; FRED AND EUNICE TEES, AND MARIE LOUISE GAY AND DAVID HOMEL, FOR THEIR SPECIAL WELCOMES IN MONTREAL; SUZANNE MORIN AT THE MCCORD MUSEUM IN MONTREAL FOR THE TIME SHE TOOK WITH MY MANY QUESTIONS; VICTOR FLEISCHER AND RAYMOND FOLLOWS AT THE MUSÉE DES POMPIERS AUXILIARES FOR THEIR TIME AND INTEREST IN THIS PROJECT; LE CENTRE

D'HISTOIRE DE MONTREAL, LE MUSÉE DU FIER MONDE, LA
BIBLIOTHÈQUE NATIONALE DU QUÉBEC, LE CHATEAU RAMEZAY,
LE MUSÉE DE MARGUERITE BOURGEOIS, LE MUSÉE
D'HOSPITALIERS DE L'HOTEL DIEU, WESTMOUNT LIBRARY IN
MONTREAL, AND ALL THE MONTREALERS WHO SPOKE FRENCH
DURING MY TIME IN THEIR CITY; THE TORONTO PUBLIC LIBRARY,
AND ESPECIALLY THE STAFF AT NORTH YORK CENTRAL; MICHAEL
BLISS, BETTINA BRADBURY, HERBERT AMES, AND EDGAR COLLARD,
FOR THEIR BOOKS AND COLUMNS THAT WERE ESPECIALLY HELPFUL
IN CONDUCTING MY RESEARCH; AND MY WRITING GROUP, LENA
COAKLEY, HADLEY DYER, WENDY LEWIS, AND PAULA WING, WHOSE
FEEDBACK ON THE MANUSCRIPT WAS, AS ALWAYS, INVALUABLE.

EMILY: BOOK ONE

ACROSS THE
JAMES BAY
BRIDGE

JULIE LAWSON

For

Charlayne Thorton-Joe

MEET EMILY

T HE YEAR IS 1896. THE PLACE IS VICTORIA, BRITISH Columbia. The young girl you're about to meet is ten-year-old Emily Murdoch.

Emily and her two younger sisters were born in the Dominion of Canada, but her parents came from England, in the 1880s. They settled in a Victoria neighbourhood called James Bay, a residential area popular with working-class, middle-class, and upper-class families. It is also an industrial area, with factories, shipyards, and an ocean dock that could accommodate large vessels.

Emily's father works in a bank, and she and her sisters enjoy a comfortable, middle-class lifestyle. Like other girls her age, Emily goes to school and church, and enjoys playing with her friends.

By 1889, Victoria was the largest and wealthiest city in the province. Its location, on the southeastern tip of

Vancouver Island, made it a commercial centre for foreign trade, and the first available seaport north of San Francisco. It housed the provincial government, the Royal Navy, and the second-largest iron-works on the Pacific coast. It was a large manufacturing centre, and boasted an assortment of activities related to forestry, fishing, sealing, agriculture, and commerce.

During Emily's ten years, the Esquimalt and Nanaimo Railway had arrived in town, electric lighting was introduced, and mail was delivered to her door twice a day—free. Recent improvements in the city water works provided residents with an abundant supply of pure water, ample for fire protection as well as domestic use. The city had a sewage system, indoor plumbing, and an expanding streetcar service.

Victoria also had a touch of the exotic. In the early 1880s, several shiploads of Chinese people were brought to British Columbia to work on the Fraser Canyon section of the new Canadian Pacific Railway. When the construction was complete, thousands settled in Victoria's Chinatown. Many found employment as cooks, servants, or gardeners in Victorian households such as Emily's.

Although Chinese New Year celebrations and funeral processions fascinated some white residents, anti-

Chinese sentiments were still the rule of the day. In 1885, the federal government introduced a fifty-dollar head tax on every Chinese person entering the country, in an attempt to control Chinese immigration.

As 1896 is ushered in, the world around Emily is beginning to change. An increasing shortage of gold had led to panic in 1893 and a worldwide financial depression had followed. Emily is unaware of the effect this might have on her family. She expects life to go on as usual—with some new friends, perhaps, and new adventures. She hopes she'll get society's latest craze—a bicycle. But what does the new year really have in store for her?

Turn the page and read on!

CHAPTER No 1

The first day of 1896 blew in with a bitter wind and the threat of snow. In spite of the cold, Emily and her younger sister Jane were happy to be outside in Beacon Hill Park.

Things were bustling at home. Ten guests would be arriving later that afternoon for the Murdochs' annual New Year's party. A few of those guests had already sent ahead their Chinese servants to help Hing prepare the dinner, and Mother and Father were making sure that everything was perfect, down to the last detail. Because the girls kept getting in the way, Mother had sent four-year-old Amelia to bed for a nap and told Jane and Emily they could go to the park and feed the ducks—provided they dressed warmly and hurried home the instant they heard the gong.

The ducks were used to the girls' weekly offerings and quickly gathered around. But when a mob of seagulls squawked in for their share, Emily would have none of it. "Shoo!" she yelled. She ran in circles, flinging her arms in an attempt to scare them away. "This is a *duck* pond!"

"Look, Em!" Jane called out. She had several of the ducks trying to eat out of her hand. "One of them's pecking my finger."

"You chase the gulls for a while and let me feed them," Emily said, racing over to her sister. She took some grain from the small bag that Jane was carrying, moved a few yards away, then crouched down and held out two handfuls. "Here, ducks! Over here!"

"Over *here!*" Jane countered. Soon they were deeply involved in a contest over who could attract the greater number.

Suddenly, the clamour of a gong echoed across the park.

"Oh, no!" Emily cried. "Is it that time already? Come on, Jane. We've got to go home." She scattered the remaining feed and grabbed her sister's hand.

Emily was used to Hing's gong. Before he'd started using it, she had always arrived late for lunch on school days. Hing had finally laid down the law. "I stand outside, beat gong when dinner ready," he'd said. "If you not here, you miss."

The gong outdid the clanging of the streetcar and could be heard throughout James Bay. The moment Emily heard it, she would stop whatever she was doing and run like the dickens. She didn't want to make Hing angry. If he was angry, there would be no lemon tarts!

No, the gong was not to be taken lightly— not on regular days, not on New Year's Day, and certainly not when Father was home.

Home was only three blocks from the park. But as the girls were nearing the end of the second block, Emily spotted something that made her forget the gong and come to an abrupt stop.

"Oh, Jane!"

"What?"

"See, on Sullivans' verandah? The bicycle." She leaned over the picket fence and sighed. "It's a Red Bird. That's what I wanted for Christmas."

"Maybe you'll get one for your birthday," Jane said. "It's not that far away." She gave Emily an encouraging smile and continued on home.

Emily stared at the bicycle. A birthday present? Jane could be right. Father had often said that a tenth birthday was extra special.

Another clanging of the gong tore her away. She could picture Father pulling out his watch, his foot tapping with impatience. Of course, once she had her bicycle, she would always be on time.

Father was waiting at the door, watch in hand. "Quickly, girls! The guests will be arriving in forty-five minutes. We want you scrubbed and polished." He smiled.

"Did you polish your gold tooth, Father?" Emily asked. "It's gleaming."

"Of course, my dear. You can't start a new year without giving everything a special shine. So off you go! And mind you don't dawdle."

"No, Father." She raced Jane upstairs to the bathroom for the required scrubbing.

Amelia, who looked as polished as a new penny, came in to supervise. "Don't forget your ears and your fingernails," she said. "Mother will check."

After their bath, they went to their room and found their best clothes neatly laid out on the bed.

Emily reached for her stockings. "Do you remember last year's party, Jane? There won't be as many people this year, but it will be even better because some *new* people are coming! They just arrived from England. Mr. Walsh works in the bank with Father. They've got one son in the Royal Navy and one son who's eleven. His name is George."

"How do you know? And you'd better hurry. I'm already dressed."

Emily put on her petticoat, then reached for her frilly white dress. "I know because they bought the house next door to Alice." Alice was Emily's closest friend.

Just then Mother came in, her silk dress swishing across the floor. "Still not ready? Oh, Emily! You know how your father likes things to run smoothly." She fastened the mother-of-pearl buttons on Emily's dress, then turned her attention to her hair.

Emily squirmed and wriggled but at last the ordeal was over: starched dress done up, long curls brushed out, red velvet sash tied around her waist, matching ribbon in her hair. After her hands and fingernails—and ears—were examined, she had only to put on her shoes and go downstairs.

One by one the guests arrived. They gathered in both the sitting room and the parlour, chatting over glasses of punch while warming themselves by the fire.

Emily waited excitedly for the newcomer, George. She wanted to show him around the house and tell him about the school he'd be attending once the holidays were over. But when he and his parents arrived, there wasn't time. Dinner was announced. The guests made their way into the dining room in a leisurely fashion and took their places at the long table.

Mother had seated George and Emily side by side.

"Your neighbour, Alice, told me all about you," Emily said.

George gave her a mischievous grin. "Her brother, Tom, told me all about *you*."

"Oh, no!" Emily giggled and hid her face so he wouldn't see her blushing.

After Father said grace, Hing brought in the plates and began to serve, helped out on this occasion by a neighbour's housemaid. The first course was oyster pie, followed by a clear soup. Then came chicken and tongue and cold boiled ham, with mixed pickles and celery, onions in cream sauce, and two types of potatoes: sweet potatoes with brown sugar, mashed potatoes with gravy. Emily noticed that George was tucking in heartily, but she was careful to save room for dessert.

Finally Hing brought in the flaming plum pudding. Emily savoured every bite, especially the hard sauce poured over top.

It was a long time to sit minding your manners. Emily didn't realize how much she'd been fidgeting until she caught Father's eye. She immediately stopped pleating her linen napkin and folded her hands in her lap. She glanced at Mother, hoping to be excused from the table, but Mother shook her head and mouthed the word "toasts."

The dreaded toasts. Emily sighed loudly and slumped in her chair, prompting another stern look from Father.

Then, at last, Father was on his feet, wineglass in hand. "The Queen!" he said. Everyone stood up, raised his glass, and repeated, "The Queen!"

Emily and George were over eight years old, so they were each given a half glass of white wine. George downed his in one gulp, then made a spectacle of himself by coughing. Emily knew better—the stuff tasted horrid—so she merely touched the glass to her lips and pretended to drink.

No sooner had the Queen been toasted than Mr. Walsh stood and proposed a toast to their hostess. Once again everyone stood and raised his glass, this time to Mother. Then it was Father's turn. Stand, raise glass, sit down. Happy New Year, good health .... And so it went, round the table, with toasts to everyone.

Emily wished she could propose a marmalade instead of a toast. A marmalade to Jane and Amelia. Or why not to George? She glanced at him and stifled a giggle. With his reddish-brown hair, perhaps she ought to propose a strawberry jam!

The toasts dragged on. At last, when Emily had had all the stands and sits she could take, Father allowed the children to be excused.

"We're going to play Happy New Year with our dolls," Jane said.

"You can play, too, Em," said Amelia. "And George can make the toasts."

Emily shook her head. "We're going to have a tour of the house."

She grabbed George's hand, taking him very much by surprise, and they made their getaway up the staircase.

She proudly showed him the new bathroom, with its indoor flush toilet and claw-foot tub. Next came the play room, where her sisters' dolls were sitting down to their New Year's feast. After a quick peek inside her parents' bedroom, they went into the room Emily shared with her sisters. It was large and bright with a window seat that overlooked the street.

"I can watch everything from here," she said. "I can see when my friends are coming, and the postman and the milkman. And what the Chinese peddlers are selling."

"Chinese peddlers?" George turned up his nose.

"Haven't you seen them? They balance a bamboo pole on their shoulders and hang a basket at each end. They go from house to house all over Victoria. Some of them sell vegetables or fish, and some collect the laundry. I can watch the streetcar, too. It's electric! It goes right down our street and stops at the next block. Wait till you hear it! The bell clangs and the overhead wires whistle and the conductor shouts hello to everyone. It takes you anywhere in the city for five cents."

Back on the main floor, they looked into the kitchen, where the Chinese servants were washing the dishes. One man paused above a vat of boiling water and caught sight of Emily.

"Em-ry!" he called out. *"Gung hey fat choy."*

"Gung hey fat choy!" she replied. "That's Hing," she told George. "He's teaching me some Chinese."

George grunted. "Don't tell me you under-stand that *hey choy* nonsense."

"It's what the Chinese say for Happy New Year. But their new year is different from ours."

"What's 'Em-ry,' then?"

"My name, silly! He calls Alice 'A-ris.'"

"Barbarians," George muttered.

"Didn't you have a Chinese servant in England?"

George gave her a horrified look. "We had English servants, of course."

"What's in this room?" He stopped before a door at the end of the hall.

"That's Father's study. We're not allowed in unless—George!"

He was already inside, gazing at a vast collection of objects displayed in a large glass cabinet. "What's all this?"

"Father's antiquities," Emily explained. "They're from the Far East. Father got some on his travels and some were gifts. See the vase with the dragon?" She pointed to a blue-and-white porcelain vase. "It only just arrived. My uncle in London sent it. Father says it's eight hundred years old."

"Is that a real dagger beside it?" George asked. "I say! It looks like a ram's head on the handle. Can I have a closer look?"

"No!" Emily cried in alarm. "What are you doing? You can't touch it!" She reached out to stop him. As she did so, her arm brushed the vase and sent it crashing to the floor.

"Oh, no!" she gasped. Her stomach churned. What would Father say?

"I don't think anyone heard," George said. "Do you?"

"I don't know." Her mouth felt so dry she could hardly speak.

"At least *I* didn't break it," George went on. "You're in for it now. Would you like me to tell your father? Might make it easier."

She shook her head, wishing she could die on the spot.

"Suit yourself," George said. "Shall we go back upstairs and spy on your sisters?" Before she could answer, he was gone.

With shaking fingers, Emily picked up the broken pieces. Part of the vase was still intact. If it were facing out . . . She propped it on the shelf and hid the other pieces in behind. It looked a little tippy, but it would have to do for now. Tonight she would not pray for a bicycle. She would pray that Father stay out of his study for a very long time.

She left the study and closed the door. As she was passing the dining room she heard her father say, "A toast—to better times."

Emily couldn't help but agree.

Her arm brushed the vase and sent it crashing to the floor. "Oh, no!" she gasped. What would Father say?

Then Father continued, "Not to put a damper on the festivities, but I cannot help worrying about this economic slump and its outcome. I fear we may have some tough times ahead."

Emily frowned. The broken vase certainly meant tough times for *her* once Father found out. But what did "tough times" mean for him and his guests? He worked in the bank, so perhaps it had to do with money. And if *that* were the case, maybe that was why she didn't get a bicycle for Christmas.

No, that couldn't be right. Father had no end of money. Like Jane said, he was saving the bicycle for her birthday. The thought made her smile . . . until she remembered the vase.

And later, when everyone was joining hands and singing "Auld Lang Syne," Emily had but one thought: How could she put it back together?

CHAPTER N° 3

As luck would have it, it snowed overnight.
Father shovelled the verandah steps and then left
right away for his usual walk to the bank. Mother
went outside with Jane and Amelia to help them
build a snowman. Emily stayed inside. With Hing
having the day off, she had the house to herself.

She had a plan, but she had to act quickly. First
she needed glue. What kind of glue worked with
porcelain? Surely not the ordinary paste she used
for paper. She needed something strong, something hard. . . . Mother's hard sauce! Mother often

made glue with flour and water but it was lumpy. The sauce was smooth. And when it was dry it went hard, like frosting on a cake.

She dashed to the kitchen and flipped through the pages of her mother's book, the *Household Companion,* until she found the recipe. Butter, powdered sugar, brandy. She put some sugar in a bowl, added the butter, and beat it into a thick, smooth paste.

She couldn't find the brandy, but she figured a colourless liquid labelled "alcohol" would do the trick. She stirred in a few drops. The smell was so horrid she decided not to taste it. Besides, her sauce was not for pudding.

She hurried into the study and removed the broken vase. There were about ten pieces, and some were rather large. Taking one piece at a time, she applied the glue to the broken edges. Then, with trembling fingers, she fit the pieces together.

She was wiping away the smudges when she heard her sisters calling at the back door. "Emily, get us a carrot! Our snowman needs a nose! And Mother says to hurry!"

"Coming!" she cried. She returned the vase to the cabinet and gave it one last look. The blue lines of the dragon matched up, and the glue appeared to be holding. Unless Father examined the vase closely, he would never know.

The snow kept Emily's mind off the vase and her father out of his study. Victoria didn't get much snow, and Emily couldn't miss the opportunity to go sledding with her friends. As for Father, as soon as he got home from work, he took the whole family to Beacon Hill Park for sleigh rides with friends and neighbours. For two afternoons and evenings the streets rang with sleigh bells instead of the clanging streetcars.

On the third night of the new year, Emily was awakened by a dreadful shaking. The whole house rocked. Windows rattled and glassware jingled. When the shaking finally stopped, Mother and Father rushed in to calm the frightened girls.

"It was an earthquake," said Father. "It's all over now."

The next day they learned that the earthquake had lasted fifteen seconds and had been felt throughout Victoria. "It was quite severe," Father told them, "but there was no serious damage."

Emily thought of the vase. If it were discovered now, they could blame the earthquake. "Did anything get broken?" she asked. "Any dishes or . . . vases?"

"Not so much as an egg cup," Mother said. "The only thing that shattered was our nerves."

"Not even the slightest crack?" Emily persisted.

Father ruffled her hair. "What a worrier you are! There wasn't the tiniest splinter."

"Our snowman got broke," Amelia said glumly.

"You can blame that on the rain," Father said. "There'll be no sleigh rides today."

Jane sniffed. "And no more snow."

"But there might be another earthquake?" Emily tried to keep her voice from sounding too hopeful.

"No, dear." Mother gave her a hug. "You'll sleep peacefully tonight."

CHAPTER N⁰ 4

"*Go on, Emily!*" *George gave her a poke.*
"Sneak up and pull his pigtail."

From her hiding place behind the hedge in front
of George's house, Emily watched the peddler jog-
trotting along the muddy street. He was a familiar
sight, dressed in dark, baggy trousers, a loose-fitting
jacket, and a wide-brimmed hat. And like the other
Chinese men, he wore his hair in a long pigtail.

"He's not going to bite you," Alice said.
"George pulled a peddler's pigtail yesterday. Tom
and I did too."

"We dare you," George went on. "If you're not too much of a scaredy-cat."

Emily frowned. She didn't want to do it. If Hing found out, he wouldn't like it one bit.

Still, she didn't take dares lightly. And as for being a scaredy-cat? They'd see about that.

She ran up behind the peddler and gave his pigtail a good hard tug. He whirled around and shouted as she fled back to the hedge.

"He sure looked mad." Alice laughed. "Did you see him shaking his fist? He probably put a curse on you."

"Where does he live?" George asked.

"In Chinatown, where else?" said Alice. "Mother says it stinks to high heaven of sharks' fins and rotten eggs."

"You must mean thousand-year-old eggs," Emily said. "They're not really that old, and they're not rotten. They're preserved. They're dark purple on the outside and green inside."

"How do you know?" said Tom.

"Hing brought me one to taste. It was good."

The others groaned with disgust. "You wouldn't catch me eating that rubbish," George said. "And I'd never set foot in Chinatown."

"Me neither," said Alice. "Would you, Em?"

"Yes!" Emily suddenly felt very bold. "In fact, I think I might go this very afternoon. And I dare all of you to come with me."

"You can't be serious," said Tom.

"Why not? I went once before, with Father. And it's not as bad as you make out. So . . . I double dare you."

Alice shook her head. "Our parents would never allow it."

"They wouldn't need to know," Emily continued, warming to her plan. "We'll ask if we can go across the bridge into town. We could even do some errands and get candy at the grocer's." When the others still hesitated, she burst out, "You're brave enough to pull a peddler's pigtail but you won't even go to Chinatown? You only have to stay a minute. I triple dare you!" She glared at George. "If you don't, I'll tell Father you went snooping into his room. When *I* told you not to!"

George rolled his eyes. "Oh, very well. Let's all go. It might be a lark. If we remember to plug our noses."

Everyone received permission for the trip to town, and shortly after lunch they were ready to go. Mother told Emily to be back for tea and to bring home some candy for her sisters. "Behave yourself," she said. "And stay on the boardwalks. The roads are a frightful mess."

A brisk walk down Birdcage Walk led them to the wooden bridge that spanned James Bay. As they stepped onto the bridge, Emily pulled a face. "Eugh! Low tide!"

"It stinks here all the time," said Alice.

A stream of foam came spewing out of the soap-works factory on the far shore. It floated onto the mud flats and mingled with the garbage and debris that people often dumped in the bay.

"I like it at high tide," said Emily. "In the summer, Father rents a rowboat and takes us under the bridge."

Once they crossed the bridge, they headed up Government Street. Horse-drawn hacks stood one behind the other, waiting for fares. The streetcar whistled by at a good ten miles an hour.

They passed the Bank of B.C. where Emily's father worked, several dry-goods stores, a clothier's, a butcher's, and the post office. When they reached the grocer's, they hurried inside for their candy. Everything was out in the open, from hams and bacon to barrels of English biscuits and enormous rounds of cheese. Emily counted out a penny's worth of lemon barley sugar sticks and butter taffy drops, making sure she had enough for her sisters.

They left the grocer's and continued up the street. But as they were crossing the Johnson

Street ravine, they heard a series of explosions that stopped them in their tracks.

"That sounds like firecrackers!" George exclaimed. "Where are they coming from?"

"Chinatown," Emily said. "We're almost there."

They reached the end of the footbridge, walked a short distance in the mud, then turned into Chinatown.

The street was crowded with Chinese people, chatting in small groups or hurrying along with their bamboo poles. A string of firecrackers, tied in tight red clusters, hung from a wooden balcony all the way down to the boardwalk below. Someone had lit the string at the lower end, and the fire was steadily popping its way to the top.

"Let's take the rest!" said George. "We can set them off in the park!" He grabbed the string and yanked it from the balcony. Then he stamped out the fire, scooped up the unlit firecrackers, and ran off.

"Stop!" someone shouted. Several men gave chase.

"Down here!" Emily cried. She ducked into a narrow brick alley, assuming the others were close behind. But when she stopped for breath, she found she was alone. Where were they? Surely they wouldn't have run off and left her.

She continued down the alley, not daring to return to the street with all the shouting going on. That George! she thought angrily. It's his fault. If I have to go home by myself . . .

The alley had begun to twist and turn, with numerous paths branching off in different directions. Emily followed one after another. Finally, with no end in sight, she realized she would have to retrace her steps.

"I hope you're satisfied, George!" she fumed. "Mr. Know-it-all!" Then anxiously, "How do I get out of here?"

Just then, who should appear but Hing.

"Em-ry?" He frowned. "What are you doing here?"

"Oh, Hing!" Her words came out in a rush. "I didn't want to pull his pigtail but they dared me.

So then I dared them to come to Chinatown, especially that George, who's always getting into trouble. First it was Father's study and the vase—and it was *his* fault I broke it! And then he stole the firecrackers. That's why we ran off. I came down the alley to hide—" A thought struck her. "Is it Chinese New Year already? Is that why there are firecrackers?"

"No, no. New Year next month. Firecrackers for open new store. To scare away evil spirits and bring good fortune."

"Oh." She gave him a worried look. "Why aren't you still at my house?" He'd been there that morning, cooking the traditional Saturday roast so they could have cold pork on Sunday. "Your half day is Sunday, isn't it? Are you sick?"

"No, no. Change half day, one time. Today—" His words were interrupted by a loud banging. "Come!" He took her hand and led her back to the street.

A large and noisy procession was moving through Chinatown. Cymbals crashed. Women

"Let's take the rest!" said
George. He grabbed the string
of firecrackers, yanked it from
the balcony, and ran off.

cried and wailed. They even held bowls under their eyes to catch the tears.

"What kind of parade is that?" Emily asked. "And why are all those people wearing white?"

"Funeral," Hing said. "Friend from home village." He told Emily he'd take her as far as the James Bay bridge, but then he would join the procession himself.

By the time they turned down Government, the street was lined with curious onlookers.

"There's Alice, up ahead," Emily said. "And Tom and George. Thank goodness, he doesn't have the firecrackers any more." She handed Hing a butter taffy drop and ran to join her friends.

CHAPTER N⁰ 5

At school on Monday, Emily was faced with a barrage of questions. "Where's your bicycle?" her classmates asked. "You said you were getting one for Christmas."

"It's going to be a birthday present," she told them.

"How do you know for sure? What kind are you getting? Will you let us ride it sometimes?"

She answered the questions as best she could, until, much to her relief, her teacher rang the bell.

As she was walking home at noon, she once again spotted the Red Bird bicycle. This time, it was leaning against the side of the Sullivans' house.

No one was about. She went over to the bicycle and touched the smooth frame. She spun the pedals and gripped the handlebars. She clambered onto the leather seat, bracing herself against the wall. Even though her feet didn't quite reach the pedals, she closed her eyes and pretended she was flying along Dallas Road with the sea breeze in her hair. It was one of the Ten Commandments not to covet anything that belonged to a neighbour, but oh, how she coveted that bicycle! Only three weeks until her birthday. Maybe Father had already bought her bicycle. Maybe he was hiding it in the bank, away from prying eyes.

When her imaginary ride was over, she hopped off and daringly rang the little bell attached to the handlebars. Its brassy tinkle reminded her that she hadn't heard Hing's gong.

She gave the bicycle one last pat and hurried on, thinking she was either very early or extremely late.

At home, she was astonished to find her sisters bickering in the breakfast room, her mother in a panic in the kitchen, and no meal in sight.

"Emily, where have you been?" Mother cried.

Without waiting for an answer, she thrust a plate of cold tongue sandwiches into Emily's hands. "Put this on the table and come back for the milk. It never rains but it pours. Today of all days, with guests coming for tea."

"It's not raining!" Amelia squealed. "Mother, you said it was raining and pouring!"

"Hush, Amelia, and eat! You, too, Jane. And Emily, you're going to be late for school."

Between mouthfuls, Emily said, "I saw a Red Bird bicycle on my way home. I hope I get the same kind for my birthday. I sat on the seat to try it out and it was almost my size. It was rather high, but I don't think it's all that difficult to lower the seat. Won't it be grand, Mother? I'll never be late, and Hing won't ever have to bang the gong again. Where is he, anyway?"

"Oh, Emily! I'm so sorry, I know how fond you are of Hing—"

"Mother, what's happened? Is he all right?"

"When's he coming back?" Jane asked.

"Hing's hurt!" Amelia began to cry.

"No, no, it's nothing like that," Mother said reassuringly. "Girls, your father dismissed Hing this morning. He acted in haste, and I'm sure he'll regret it and make amends, but meanwhile—oh, Amelia, let Jane pour your milk, you're going to knock it over—meanwhile, the ladies will be here sharp at two o'clock and nothing's prepared!"

Emily had never seen her mother in such a state. "I'll stay home and help," she offered.

"Me too!" said Jane. "If Emily misses school, can I?"

"No, Jane."

"That's not fair!" Jane pounded the table and knocked over her milk.

"Now look what you've done! Emily, give me a hand, please."

The next several minutes were filled with crying and confusion. But soon Amelia was in bed for a nap and Jane was on her way back to school. Mother mixed batter for scones. And after clearing the table and wiping the spilt milk, Emily was set to work making egg salad sandwiches.

"What about Hing?" she asked as she sliced the bread. "Will he be here tomorrow? He promised he'd make lemon tarts tomorrow. Why did Father dismiss him? Mother—"

"Emily, please! It's all very distressing, and I'll explain in due course, but now is simply not the time. Oh, dear, look at the bread! We want thin straight across, not sloping. And for goodness' sake, don't slice your finger."

Before long, the thick-and-thin sandwiches were on a plate, the scones were in the oven, and the guests were sipping tea in the parlour.

Emily was filling a cut-glass bowl with straw-berry preserves to go with the scones when she heard Hing's name. Curious, she crept down the hall and, sucking on a spoonful of preserves, put her ear to the parlour door. She was just in time to hear her mother say, ". . . discovered it broken and dismissed him this morning."

Emily gasped in disbelief. Hing could not have been dismissed because of the vase. He knew that *she* was responsible. Surely he would have said something.

"The blue and white porcelain vase," her mother went on. "Yesterday afternoon, before we went to the church social, I asked Hing to do a thorough cleaning in Robert's study. There's been the most peculiar smell of rubbing alcohol. Well, as he was cleaning the shelves in the display case, he must have dropped the vase."

"You can't trust them." Emily recognized the voice of George's mother, Mrs. Walsh. "I know it's the custom in Victoria, but I certainly wouldn't have a Chinaman in my house."

"But he's an excellent servant!" Mother exclaimed. "Ten years he's been with us, since

Emily was a baby, and not a speck of trouble."

"What did he have to say for himself?"

"Nothing. He remained absolutely silent."

Emily's stomach lurched. Hing had been dismissed because of her, and he hadn't let on . . .

"Who else could it have been?" Mother continued. "The girls are forbidden to go into the study."

"You should have hired an English servant from the start," Mrs. Walsh said. "They're much more reliable."

"Nonsense!" someone retorted. "Not any of the girls I've had. They stay for a month, then they're off getting married. No, the Orientals are definitely the best, provided you train them properly and keep an eye on them. I was saying the other day . . . excuse me, Anne, I don't mean to be rude, but is something burning?"

"Oh, mercy!" Emily bolted back to the kitchen, her mother close behind. She flung open the oven door and gagged as smoke billowed into the room. Then she grabbed the oven mitts and pulled out the blackened mess. There would be no scones served with thick cream and strawberry preserves today.

"Whatever were you thinking?" Mother spoke sharply, but sounded more exasperated than angry.

Emily tried to keep her voice from trembling. "Mother, I'm sorry. I promise I'll clean up, but right now I have to go back to school because I've forgotten something important."

"Your father will hear about this!"

"I know," Emily said as she grabbed her coat and ran out. "And I'll explain everything."

First, she had to find Hing.

CHAPTER Nº 6

Emily's plan was simple. She would go to Chinatown, find Hing, and take him home with her. Once Father learned the truth about the vase, he'd likely give Emily a sound thrashing—but at least he'd give Hing back his job.

When she got to Chinatown, she turned down the same alley she'd gone into before, found the same lane, and recognized the spot where Hing had unexpectedly appeared. The problem was, where exactly had he come from?

It was different in this hidden part of Chinatown. There were chicken coops, barking dogs, lines of washing, and gardens with winter vegetables. The tightly packed buildings bulged in on each other, sometimes three storeys high.

She walked through a courtyard and down another alley, only to reach a dead end. She tried a different route but ended up in another courtyard.

Passersby gave her curious looks. "Hing?" she asked. "Do you know Hing?" No one could help.

With a growing sense of panic, she wandered through the maze, from dead end to dead end, one courtyard to another. There were too many staircases, too many doorways. Faces peered out of windows, smoke rose from chimneys. Inside the squalid rooms, lamps were being lit. It would soon be dark. And it was starting to rain.

Just then, a peddler stepped out of a doorway. Emily was about to approach when she recognized him as the man whose pigtail she had pulled. She shuddered. She couldn't ask *him* for help. He'd think she was up to more mischief and put another curse on her. If he so much as saw her . . .

She turned too quickly, stumbled over a heap of refuse, and fell onto a jagged pile of bricks. "Oh, mercy!" A sob welled up in her throat. It was raining hard now, the wind cut through to her bones, and her hands and knees smarted horribly.

"Em-ry?"

The familiar voice made her giddy with relief.

"Oh, Hing, I'm so sorry! That vase . . . I should have told Father right away instead of trying to hide it, and now you've lost your job. So will you come home with me? I'll tell Father and he'll hire you back—" A dreadful thought struck her. What if Hing had taken another position? What if he didn't want to come back? She burst into tears. "Oh, please!"

"Come." He led her to a door a few steps away and ushered her inside a cramped and dingy room. After clearing a space for her to sit down, he poured her a cup of tea. "Drink," he said. "Then we go home and explain."

She thanked him, then picked up the cup and frowned. The tea didn't look like proper tea; there were leaves floating on top. But she remembered her manners and took a sip. It had a slightly bitter, but pleasant taste, and it warmed her right through.

"Green tea," Hing said. "You like?"

"Yes. Thank you." As she drank the tea, she took in her surroundings—the rough pieces of furniture, a wood stove, shelves with cracked and mismatched china. On a crate beside the narrow bed she noticed a studio portrait of a young Chinese woman seated with two small boys.

"Who are they?" she wondered.

"Wife and sons." Hing smiled proudly.

"Are they in Victoria too?"

Hing's expression changed. He told Emily how he'd come to Canada in 1883 to work on the railway, hoping to earn enough money to send for his family. Two years later he'd succeeded. He'd then returned to China and spent many months visiting friends and relatives and telling them about the land they called Gold Mountain.

It was difficult to follow everything he said. He spoke slowly and all his *l*'s came out as *r*'s. But his story fascinated Emily. It was like a fairy tale, only real. Even though there was no happy ending. Hing and his family had packed their belongings for Gold Mountain only to discover that the government in Canada had established a head tax. Every Chinese entering the country had to pay fifty dollars. Hing could only afford to pay for himself.

The opportunities in Gold Mountain were so much greater than those in his homeland, he had left his wife and sons and returned to Victoria. He'd promised to send for them as soon as he could save enough money to cover their head tax.

"You must miss them," said Emily.

"I have daughter, too," he said sadly. "Born in Year of Dog. Ten years old. Like you."

"*Almost* ten," Emily reminded him. "Is she pretty, like your wife?"

"I never see her. No picture. But I think yes, she very pretty."

Hing told Emily how he'd
come to Canada, hoping
to earn enough money to
send for his family.

Emily didn't understand why Hing, who'd been working in Victoria for ten years, still hadn't saved enough money to send for his family. It would be rude to ask, but she couldn't help but wonder.

"Getting late," Hing said. "We go now."

Emily thought about his story all the way home. To think Hing had a wife and children she'd never even heard about . . . He must miss them dreadfully. And to leave Emily's cozy house, night after night, for that horrid little room . . .

She wondered if her parents knew. Well, as soon as the vase business was settled and Hing was back at work, she'd tell them. And when Father learned how lonely Hing was, he'd pay him a higher wage. Then Hing would be able to bring his family to Canada and the story would have a happy ending. Especially when Hing saw his daughter for the very first time.

CHAPTER No. 7

Father did not look pleased when Emily came into the house. He held out his pocket watch and said sternly, "Do you see what time it is? Mother and I have been frantic. What do you have to say for yourself?"

Emily glanced over her shoulder at Hing, waiting in the doorway. Then she bowed her head and stammered, "I had to find Hing, Father. He got fired because of me. Because I broke the vase. And I was afraid to tell you."

Her parents looked at her with shocked expressions. Before they could say anything, she rushed on.

"It was at the New Year's party and George went into your study and he wanted to see the dagger. I tried to stop him . . ." She swallowed hard to force back the tears. "I knocked over the vase and I glued it back together. Then Hing got blamed and you sent him away, and the whole time he never said it was me, even though he knew. Oh, please, Father! Please hire him back! He's got a whole family in China and a little girl—"

"That's enough for now, Emily," Father said. "Wait for me in the study. Mother and I will speak to you shortly."

The list seemed endless. Emily stood before her father, head hung in disgrace, as Mother gave a full account of the day's disasters.

"I left her with the simple task of keeping an eye on the scones. Instead, she left the kitchen and dripped strawberry preserves on the carpet. Then she stepped in it and tracked it down the hall. The scones were burnt to cinders. And what does she do then? She flies out with a story about forgetting something at school. As for the rest! Going into the study, breaking the vase—admittedly, it was an accident—and failing to say anything . . ." Mother shook her head.

Father sighed. "You did a great wrong by not telling us about the vase. But you've put things right in an admirable way. Except for the mess in the hall and kitchen, and you'll clean that up tomorrow." He then sent her sobbing to her room.

"Don't cry, Em," Jane said, giving her a hug. "Father won't stay mad for long, and you'll still get your bicycle. And—don't tell, but I was listening outside the door and I know Hing's coming back first thing tomorrow."

Emily squeezed Jane's hand. The thought of Hing in his lonely room, with no family close by for comfort, made her cry even harder.

The next evening, Emily decided to put another plan into action.

"Father," she said, "when you and Mother came to Canada did you pay a head tax?"

"Head tacks?" Amelia looked puzzled. "That would hurt."

"Not those tacks," Emily said. "Tax like what you pay. Isn't that right, Father? Did you have to pay it?"

"What? I'm sorry, dear. What did you say?"

She repeated the question.

"Englishmen paying a head tax? Certainly not!"

"Oh. But . . . I heard people had to pay fifty dollars to come into Canada."

"Only the Chinese."

"Will they always have to pay the fifty dollars?"

"Hmm? Oh. The fifty dollars. No . . ."

Emily's face lit up. Wait till she told Hing!

Then Father continued, "It's very likely the head tax will be raised to one hundred dollars. Possibly for the best. There's enough unemployment as it is."

Oh, no. Hing would have to act quickly or pay an even higher tax.

"Father, I was wondering if you could—"

"Hush, Emily!" Mother said. "Can't you see your father's tired? You girls may be excused."

Emily sighed. Her request for Hing's raise would have to wait.

"Happy birthday, Em!" Jane and Amelia pounced on their sister. She kissed them both and ran downstairs to the breakfast room.

"Happy birthday, dear." Father ruffled her hair. "How does it feel to be ten years old?"

"It feels grown up! Enough to cycle around the world."

Mother laughed. "You'll have to wait another few years for that. Meanwhile, sit down and eat your breakfast. Father has a surprise."

"Yes, indeed," he said. "I want you to walk to

213

the bank with me this morning."

"The whole way?" She often accompanied him as far as the James Bay bridge, but going all the way to the bank was unusual.

"Yes, my dear." He flashed his gold tooth in a smile. "The whole way."

Emily looked at her parents' faces and knew that she was right. Her bicycle had to be at the bank.

But it wasn't a bicycle that awaited her.

"Here you are, Emily," Father said. "Your very own passbook. This is your account number, and you can see that I've started you off with five whole dollars."

Emily managed a smile. She mustn't appear ungrateful. Besides, it was early yet. The bicycle would likely appear at supper, along with her birthday cake and other presents.

"Where's your bicycle?" Alice asked when Emily arrived at school. "You said you were getting one for your birthday."

"It's coming later," she said.

"That's what you said at Christmas," Tom pointed out. "And you still haven't got it."

"You're not really getting a bicycle at all, are you?" George said. "You're just putting on airs. Father says they're very dear. But even so, I'm sure to get one this summer."

Emily tossed her head. "Well, I'm sure to get one this afternoon."

After school she searched her yard, the wood-shed, and the verandah. A search inside, from attic to cellar, yielded nothing. But the day was far from over.

After supper Hing brought out the birthday cake. Emily closed her eyes, made the same wish she'd been making all year, and blew out the candles. Then Mother brought in her presents. A blue velvet dress. An album for photographs. And something rolled up in brown paper and tied with string.

"Open it, Em!" Jane squirmed with excitement as Emily unrolled the paper. "It's your wish come true."

When Emily saw Jane's gift, her eyes brimmed with tears. It was a drawing of a bicycle, every detail perfect, right down to the bell on the handlebars. Beside it was a smiling little girl meant to be Emily.

"I sketched it in my art class before Christmas," Jane said. "Do you like it?"

"I love it, Jane. I'll hang it in our room straight away." She gave her a hug, then ran upstairs so Jane wouldn't see her crying.

A short time later, Father came in. He patted Emily's shoulder, then took the drawing and tacked it above the bed.

"I know you had your heart set on a real bicycle," he said. "But do you remember our New Year's party, and how we had fewer guests than usual? And how we didn't have a turkey? Well, the fact is, money is rather tight at the moment. As soon as things get better, I promise you'll have your bicycle."

Emily sniffed sadly. "Even if I'm very old, like sixteen?"

"Even if you're a grouchity old thing like me."

"You're not all that grouchity, Father."

He smiled, then reached for his handkerchief and wiped away her tears. "You know, Hing tells me that in a few days it's Chinese New Year. Would you like to go to Chinatown and see the celebration?"

"Oh, yes!" She grinned. "And since it's a new year, you'll have to polish your gold tooth."

"That's my girl! Now, let's go down and finish your cake."

Before going downstairs, Emily patted her bicycle picture and made a wish for better times.

CHAPTER N.º 9

At breakfast on the morning of Chinese New Year, Hing gave Emily two red scrolls decorated with tiny mirrors, paper flowers, and multicoloured tassels. "Hang on bedposts. Keep away bad spirits. Good luck for three little girls, all year. This year," he went on, "is Year of Monkey."

"In China, does every year have a different animal?" Emily wondered.

"Oh, yes. And every animal means different character. You same as my girl, born in Year of Dog. And Dog Year people . . . oh, my. Can be selfish. Very stubborn. But also, Dog Year people know what is right and fair." He gave her a warm smile.

"Hing," Father said, "in honour of your New Year, you may leave at noon today. And take the whole day off tomorrow."

"Thank you." Hing clasped his hands and bowed. "If I may . . . I take Em-ry to Chinese theatre tomorrow?"

"Oh, Father!" Emily exclaimed. "Please say yes!"

Her parents exchanged glances. Then Father said, "Of course. As long as Hing brings you home in time for tea."

Emily hugged herself with excitement. Tomorrow, the theatre. And today, Chinese New Year!

Hundreds of people turned out for the celebration. Chinatown echoed with the clash of cymbals and the bursting of firecrackers. Bright red banners flew from shop windows. Enormous paper lanterns dangled from balconies and lampposts. Wealthy merchants, dressed in their finest silks, offered wine, nuts, and fruit to the visitors who stopped by their shops. Emily's family received one warm welcome after another.

Every merchant gave each of the girls a small red envelope containing a five-cent piece. *"Lai see,"* one merchant explained. "Lucky money. The more we give away, the more luck we get. It's a tradition."

Emily thought it was a grand idea. She waved to two Chinese children clutching their *lai see* envelopes and called out, *"Gung hey fat choy!"* The girls covered their mouths and giggled, but their mother returned Emily's greeting.

"What will you do with your lucky money, Em?" Jane asked. "I'm going to buy some new coloured pencils. May I, Father?"

"Certainly."

"I'm going to buy a pony," said Amelia.

"It will have to be a very small pony." Father chuckled. "How about you, Emily?"

"I'll put it in my new bank account. And save it up for a bicycle."

He looked very pleased.

The Chinese theatre was nothing like the posh Victoria Opera House. Even getting there was an adventure. Emily took Hing's hand as they walked through a maze of alleys, along a narrow passageway, and up a flight of stairs. At the top, they entered a large, dimly lit room filled with benches. One end of the room served as the stage and was set up with the strangest musical instruments Emily had ever seen. Their sounds were even stranger.

The play had already started when Hing and Emily sat down, and she quickly realized that to follow the story, she had to use her imagination. When a chair was placed on the stage, for example, Hing said, "Mountain." Later, when she asked about two chairs, he said, "House." She was astonished to learn that the actors were always men. Even the women's roles were played by men speaking in high-pitched voices.

And the audience! They fell asleep, coughed and snored, chatted to friends. They stretched their legs and walked across the stage. There was even a group of men playing some kind of clicking game in the back. All this while the play was going on. And the actors didn't even mind!

The best part was that the merchants were still handing out lucky money. There weren't many children at the theatre, but those who were there, including Emily, had a growing pile of red envelopes on their laps.

She was surprised when Hing said it was time to go. "It's not over," she said.

Every merchant gave each of the girls a small red envelope containing a five-cent piece. "Lai see," one merchant explained. "Lucky money."

"Play goes on and on and on," he explained. "People come and go. Now time for tea."

They left the theatre and walked out into the sunlight. It was cold and clear, a fine February day, bursting with the sound of firecrackers.

"Will your daughter have firecrackers in China?" Emily asked.

Hing smiled. "Oh, yes! Big firecrackers. Lots of noise!"

"And lucky money?"

"Not much money. Village poor. Maybe little bit."

"I could send her some of mine."

"No, no. You keep."

Half and half, Emily decided. As they walked across the James Bay bridge, she pictured Hing's little girl opening the package from Victoria and finding a *lai see* envelope filled with Canadian coins. She wouldn't be able to spend them, so she'd have to save them for when she came here. In the meantime, she'd have extra luck, and so would Emily.

She'd still save *some* of her New Year's money for a bicycle. As for the rest, Father would understand.

She gave a little skip, realizing how lucky she was that *her* father was not off in some distant land. He was just around the corner, waiting for her to come home.

PENELOPE: BOOK ONE

TERROR IN THE
HARBOUR

SHARON E. McKAY

To Nichole,
the best of big sisters

MEET PENNY

T HIS IS THE STORY OF PENNY, THE ELDEST DAUGHTER
in a family of three girls. Penny's mother died a
year ago. Now, Penny cares for her two little sisters
while keeping up with her schoolwork. Penny's father
is very serious about schoolwork, although most people
think that women don't need much education to have
babies and keep house.

It's 1917, and the Great War in Europe has been
going on for three long years. Halifax is bursting at the
seams with soldiers going to, and coming from, the war.
Penny is often down at the docks, as her father has his
office there. She has watched young, eager soldiers
board the ships that will take them across the Atlantic.
But Penny has also seen badly wounded men coming
off the ships. Some with no arms, no legs; many leave
the ships on stretchers; all look sad and broken.

It's not only the soldiers in Europe that must defend Canada. Penny's teacher says that the people of Halifax must be on their guard too. German submarines lurk beneath the frigid waters of the Atlantic Ocean. Their intent is to torpedo ships carrying supplies and soldiers.

This morning, Penny has other things on her mind, mostly getting her little sisters over to the neighbour's house and not getting in trouble at school for being late, again! But something terrible will happen this day, something so horrifying, that Penny's life, and the lives of those around her, will be changed in the blink of an eye.

CHAPTER N<u>o</u> 1

Penny pulled her nightcap down over her ears, the quilt up to her chin, and burrowed deep under the blankets. Except for Emily's murmuring on the other side of the bed, and Maggie's squeaky baby sounds from her cradle, all was quiet.

The sun would be up soon. The curtains would have to be pulled back if the morning light was to fill the room. But it was so cold! Penny dithered, counted to three, crawled over Emily, leapt out of bed, sped across the room, and flung back the curtains. Hopping from one foot to the other, she pressed her nose against the frosty glass. It was black as pitch outside. The cobbled stones of Macara Street shimmered beneath the beam of a street light. It was December 6, and it still hadn't snowed. Two soldiers on horseback clomped on by. Soldiers were a common enough sight, since Wellington Barracks was just down the road. "They must be cold too," Penny thought, as she hurled herself back into bed and plunged under the covers to wait for daylight.

The back door downstairs squeaked. Papa was up and about. Penny could hear him fill up the scuttle with coal and toss it into the kitchen stove. Then the kettle landed on the stovetop with a thud. Now, Penny thought, Papa would wind Mama's clock, which stood on the mantel over the fire. Papa gave the clock three sharp grinds. Right on time! Penny giggled. You could know a lot about the world, if you were very still, if you listened hard enough.

It didn't take long for the heat from the stove to rise up and warm the bedroom. Penny loved their bedroom but the kitchen was the nicest room in the house, and their house was the nicest house in Halifax, no, in the world! She had helped Mama paint and wall paper the kitchen and the parlour too. They had made it a warm, welcoming home.

Papa had never liked it when Mama did heavy work. Said it wasn't fitting, her being a lady and all. "A lady?" Mama had teased him. "Since when has moving a paintbrush back and forth been considered heavy work?" She used to say that she was the happiest person in Halifax, and if he kept on at her, he would only make her miserable. Then he'd laugh too. Sometimes he'd swing Mama around the kitchen and her long blond hair would unravel from the bun at the back of her head and fall onto her shoulders. Emily had been littler then, like Maggie was now. Back then, Maggie had just been a lump in Mama's tummy.

A lady. Penny thought on that. Mama had come from an important family in Halifax. Mama's papa had been rich, but he was dead now. Mama's own mother, Penny's grandmother, was still alive, although she had moved to a grand house in Montreal just after Mama married Papa. Penny was named after her Grandmother Penelope. She shuddered. It was a silly, old-fashioned name. What she wouldn't give to be called Lily or May. Besides, Grandma Penelope had never even acknowledged her existence.

Papa's family lived across the sea in Ireland, all except his sister in Toronto. The only family Penny really knew was Aunt Colleen, Mama's cousin. Aunt Colleen had a brother named Robert. He drove a great big automobile. He said that she should call him Robert, not Uncle Robert. He said uncles were all old, stodgy fellows with moustaches. He was young and far too good-looking. He made her laugh. But it was Aunt Colleen she remembered most. Penny whispered the name in the dark. *Collll-eeeee-nnnn*. It rolled off her tongue just right. After Mama had married Papa, no one from Mama's family would talk to her, no one except Aunt Colleen and Robert. Then

Aunt Colleen had moved to Montreal to live with Grandmother Penelope.

Penny heard Papa open a cupboard door, close it again and take the kettle off the stove. He'd be making himself a mug of tea before he left for work. Papa worked hard. He had to, he said. Halifax was booming what with all the war work. Papa had his own business. He was an (Penelope paused to think of the words) independent contractor. That was right. He built the insides of buildings, the innards he said. He always laughed when he said that. But Papa didn't laugh so much now, not since Mama died.

Tips of morning light began to push back the night sky. Soon Papa would be out the door and she'd not see him again until nightfall. Then she had an idea. If she hurried she could make Papa breakfast. Penny flipped back the covers and swung her legs over the side of the bed. Emily grunted and curled up like a cooked shrimp. While one hand reached for her robe, Penny's toes searched the floor very carefully for her slippers. Emily was only five years old and didn't always push the po back under the bed.

"Penny, where are you going?" Emily mumbled from the other side of the bed.

"Don't wake up," Penny whispered, "it's too early."

"I'm cold," she murmured.

"Hush, now. You'll wake the baby. Go back to sleep."

Penny cast an eye over to Maggie's cradle. Her fat little feet were already touching the end. It was time she went into a proper crib. Maggie's first birthday wasn't far off. But how would they be able to celebrate knowing that it was the same day Mama died?

With her robe tied firmly around her, Penny yanked off her bed cap and looped an old, frayed ribbon around her long hair. Almost instantly strands of hair came loose. "Oh drat," she sighed in frustration. She hated her hair. It never did what she wanted it to do. It was long, almost to her waist, and it was red! "Auburn," Papa called it. "Beautiful Irish hair." It didn't seem fair that both Maggie and Emily had Mama's soft blond hair, and Mama's pretty looks, too.

There was nothing Penny liked about her looks. Mrs. Hanson, the lady who lived two doors down and cared for Maggie and Emily while Penny went to school, said that she was "a long drink of water." Then she'd say to anyone who'd listen, "And would ya' look at the child's colouring! A ghost has more to say for itself."

It was true, she was skinny, bony like a bicycle, all knobs and spokes. And, to top it off, she had green eyes! "Irish eyes," Papa said. Ireland, Penny grumbled, had to be filled with funny-looking girls.

Penny crept out of the bedroom, padded down the stairs and walked into the kitchen.

"Morning, Papa."

"Sure, darlin', it's too early. Back to bed with you." Papa spoke kindly. His smile went all the way up to his eyes.

"But I want to make you some breakfast." Penny reached into the larder and pulled out a basket of eggs.

Mrs. Hanson was always saying, "That man is too thin. He needs fattening up."

"I've made the porridge, that will do me right," Papa insisted.

Mama's clock struck the quarter hour.

Even if she couldn't make him breakfast Penny didn't want to go back to bed. She hardly ever had Papa to herself. Then she saw it.

"What's that?" Penny pointed to a large, brown box on the kitchen table.

"I was just about to put that away but . . ." Papa dithered. He pushed back a shock of salt-and-pepper hair and grinned. "No reason why you can't have it now."

"For me?" Penny all but threw herself on the

box. It wasn't even her birthday, and Christmas was weeks away!

"Easy now." He smiled again as he picked up his tea and eased himself into the rocking chair by the stove.

Penny tore off the top of the box and peered inside. Carefully, as carefully as if she were unwrapping the finest china, Penny folded back the tissue paper. Her breath all but left her.

"Papa!" This was too much! Too expensive. Too pretty. Too everything!

"It's time you had a proper dress. Your mother would have wanted you to have it," said Papa, his voice barely above a whisper.

"But a store-bought dress!" Penny lifted the dress out of the box and held it against her. It was blue, the colour of Mama's eyes, and belted just below the waist, with a bit of lace at the throat. It was a lady's dress.

"There's more." Papa pointed to the box. "Underthings and all. The saleslady said you'd be needing them." For reasons Penny didn't quite understand, Papa turned pink.

Penny peered back into the box and touched the petticoat.

"You'll be needing a hat, and shoes, but those will have to be fitted proper," said Papa as he took a sip of his tea.

A thought started to creep into her mind. What was it for? Why would she be needing a store-bought dress? She had two dresses as it was, and a dress for church. That was more than most girls her age had. And then she knew, and the knowledge made her knees tremble. Penny pitched the dress back in the box.

"What's wrong? Don't you like it?" Papa asked, his voice rising.

Penny spun around. It was all she could do not to shout.

"What's it for?" Her eyes brimmed with tears.

"Oh, Penny." Papa leaned back into the rocker. With a long, slow breath he said, "I've received a letter from your grandmother."

That's it! She was right. He meant to send her

Penny lifted the dress out of the box and held it against her. It was blue, the colour of Mama's eyes. It was a lady's dress.

away. He meant her to go and live with Grandmother Penelope in Montreal. Tears bubbled up and slid down her face. Her lips quivered.

"I won't go!" The words spilled out of her with such force that she stumbled forward and gripped the edge of the table. "Why? Why do you want me to go?"

"Come here, love." Papa held out his arms.

"No! You don't love me." Her words hung in the air like laundry on the line, going nowhere, just hanging.

"Penny."

"No. No." Penny thumped down onto a kitchen chair and covered her face with her hands.

"Ach, darlin', hear me out," Papa said softly. "You're a beautiful wee girl. A father never had a more lovely daughter. And I love ya' more than life itself. But you have so much ahead of you, school, maybe university. Your mother and I talked about our daughters going to the university. Sure, can ya' think on that, what it would mean for a man like myself to have educated daughters? But here, livin' like this . . ."

"Like what?" Penny interrupted. "Mama loved this house. It's a fine house."

Penny looked past her father and caught the edge of a roll of blueprints that were on top of the kitchen cupboards. They were for the house Papa had been going to build for Mama. It would have been the most beautiful house in Halifax, Papa said so. If only Mama hadn't died and Maggie hadn't been born. Tears spilled down Penny's face.

"Penny, listen to me." Papa braced himself as though he was trying to steel himself against a north wind. "You're doing work meant for a grown woman, taking care of babies, running a house. It's not right. You should be living with someone who can tell you what a young girl needs to know, about woman things. And now, with your grandmother's letter . . ." Papa ran his hands through his hair. "Your Aunt Colleen is in Montreal. You like her, don't you? Sure, your own mother loved her dearly. And your grandmother says that you'll go to a good girls' school. You'll be raised like a lady. You'll meet fine people in Montreal."

"What about Maggie and Emily? Who will take care of them?" Penny glared at her father with marble-hard eyes.

"Mrs. Hanson will, same as she does now. Business is good," Papa carried on. "Soon I'll be able to afford help full time. Someone to come in like, and take care of the house too."

"You'll get married again. That's what Mrs. Hanson says. She says that Margie Flynn has her cap set on you." Penny's words came out in sputters.

Papa laughed. To Penny it felt like a slap in the face.

"Oh my love, is that what you think? That I'm getting rid of you to marry someone?" Papa stopped laughing and looked at her steadily. "Come here."

Slowly she walked over to her father and crumpled into his lap. He rocked her back and forth, as though she were a baby and not all of ten years old.

"When your mother came into my life I thought that I'd been kissed by an angel. She was the most beautiful woman I had ever seen."

Penny nodded. Mama used to tell the story as though it were a fairytale. She'd make it sound as though she'd been a prisoner princess locked up in a castle, and only Papa's love had set her free.

"There I was, a man just starting out, an Irishman at that. I was doing work on a grand house. Most grand folks don't take too kindly to the Irish."

Penny nodded again. It was true. Even in the street they lived on, she heard people say "the dirty Irish." Why? Papa wasn't dirty.

"Poor folk and posh folk don't mix, you know that. And all I had to offer her was my heart. But it was enough. She was as kind and as good as she was lovely," Papa whispered. "Penny darlin', if I have one wish for my girls it's that you three find the love your mother and I had. Marry again?

Where on God's earth would I find someone who could hold a candle to her?"

It was then that Penny realized how lonely he must be.

"Papa, I miss her too."

"I know you do, my darlin'. But she's here. I know that she's lookin' out for us." Papa gave her a hug just as Mama's clock struck five. "There now, the men will be waiting on me. Sure, it wouldn't do for the boss to come in late, now would it?" Papa kissed the top of Penny's head and eased her up onto her feet. "You go to your bed now. Run along."

Penny struggled to stand up. She was bone-weary, as though the day had already been spent.

Papa put on his winter jacket, wrapped a muffler around his throat and pulled on his gloves. "We'll talk more tonight, all right?"

There was nothing Penny could do but nod.

Papa opened the door and was gone.

She ran her hand over the soft wool dress. Just think, Papa had picked it out just for her. It wasn't the dress's fault that she had to go away. But nothing was settled, not yet.

Penny gathered up the box and climbed the stairs. She hung the dress on the outside of the wardrobe so that she could see it from her bed.

Light streamed up over the horizon. If she strained she could look out the window and see the sun rising over the Eastern Passage. There was mist in the harbour but that would soon fade away. It would be a beautiful day. Penny covered Maggie's fat feet with the blanket and, slipping off her robe and slippers, crawled back into bed. She put her arm around Emily and pulled the sleeping child in close. Her little body was warm and comforting.

"I love you, Emily. I don't want to leave you. I don't want to leave this house."

Sleep came unbidden.

"Penny. PEN-EEEEEEEY!"

Billy, Mrs. Hanson's boy, stood outside on the cobblestone road and yelled up at Penny's bedroom window.

"PEN-EEEEEE. GET UP!"

Penny bolted up in bed.

"PEN-EEEEEE!" Billy yelled for the third time.

The time! What time was it?

"Penny, what's wrong?" Emily murmured, just as baby Maggie let out a wail.

"PEN-EEEEEEE!"

Billy Hanson, the most spoiled boy in the world, on account of his being the only boy in a household of five sisters, stood in his best winter coat and Buster Brown suit (and it wasn't even Sunday) and kept yelling his fool head off.

"Put your slippers on," said Penny to Emily as she leapt out of bed. "Billy," she yelled towards the window. "Hold on." And then, plop!

"Ohhh," Penny moaned, "the po!"

Its contents splattered all over the floor as the pot spun across the room.

"Ohhh," Penny moaned again. "Oh no."

"Penny, you spilled the piss-pot!" Emily sat up and giggled.

"The what? Who taught you that?" Penny scowled. But she knew, she absolutely knew! "It was Billy Hanson, wasn't it?" She shook with indignation as Emily's bottom lip quivered. "It's a very rude word, Emily. What would Papa say? What would Mama say?"

"I'm sorry, Penny." Emily sniffed as she rubbed her eyes with two balled-up fists.

"Sorry isn't good enough."

"PEN-EEEEEEE!"

"Stop it!" Penny leapt over the mess, flung open the window and stared down at Billy Hanson's miserable, good-for-nothing face. "Billy Hanson, if you don't stop yelling this minute I am going to give you your own head in your hands to play with." If she could have reached him, Penny would have throttled him right on the spot.

"Mama says that you are going to be late for school," Billy called back in a most self-satisfied way.

Penny leaned out the window and saw all the Hanson sisters walking down the street towards school. How? How could she have overslept?

"Tell her that I will have Maggie and Emily there as fast as I can." Penny slammed the window shut.

"Penny, Maggie's nappy smells bad." As if on cue, Maggie kicked off her blanket and let out a wail.

"She will have to wait." Penny flung Emily a pair of stockings and knickers. "Put them on, and hurry!"

Using the water from the water jug, and towels far too good for the purpose, Penny set to work cleaning the floor. She'd have to give it a real scrub when she got back from school.

Penny then pulled on her own stockings, knickers, woollen chest protector, wool skirt, blouse, and sweater.

"Pen-eee, I'm cold." Emily stomped her feet.

"Here." Penny braided her hair into one fat plait and tossed Emily the rest of her clothes. "Take them down to the kitchen and dress in front of the stove." Her heart sank. The kitchen fire would be out by now.

Penny heaved Maggie up onto her hip and almost gagged. How could a baby smell this bad?

She grabbed a nappy and new clothes for the baby, and thought about school. She'd miss morning prayers, the second time this month.

"Emily, put your slippers on. Come on."

With Maggie fussing and struggling in her arms, Penny thumped down the stairs, charged into the kitchen and plunked Maggie down in her chair. She peered into the stove. One red ember stood out from all the other crusty, grey coals. A little paper and kindling and she'd have it going again.

It took hardly any time to get Maggie put right, and set the kettle to boil, and reheat the porridge that Papa had left in the saucepan, and button up Emily's dress and jumper. There was nothing she couldn't handle, nothing she couldn't do.

Penny spooned the porridge into two bowls and plopped one in front of Emily. "Eat!" She glared at the five-year-old before turning to the baby. "Come on, Maggie, open wide." A spoonful of glob missed Maggie's mouth entirely and dangled from her chin. "Oh Maggie, please be a good girl." Penny jammed another spoonful of porridge into Maggie's mouth.

The back door opened and in fell Billy Hanson.

"Did ya' see it?" He was breathless, but nine-year-old irritating boys often are.

"You taught Emily a rude word. Go away." Penny fed Maggie another spoonful.

"What word?" Billy asked. There had been many.

"I'm not repeating it. Come on, Maggie, open up," Penny pleaded.

"Piss-pot!" said Emily. She was just trying to help, really she was.

"Emily!" This was all too much.

"Never mind that. Come and see the smoke!" Mud from Billy's feet flew in all directions. "Down at the harbour. Maybe ten ships crashed! Maybe twenty!" He was positively beaming. Nothing like a disaster to make a small boy happy.

"Don't be silly. And look at your shoes!" Penny glared down at the floor, then up at the clock. It was almost nine! Mr. Shirley was the meanest teacher in Halifax. She'd be in some trouble now.

Billy picked up one foot, then the other, and examined each with interest. Yep, there was mud on his shoes all right.

"Billy Hanson, look at the mess you are making. Get out! You are the silliest boy in Halifax, and shouldn't you be in school?" Another glob of porridge went into Maggie's porridge-splattered face.

"Mama said I could wait for you," declared Billy-the-Pain.

Penny sighed. Mrs. Hanson was just making sure that her precious Billy didn't go near the Fowlie house. They had the diphtheria. The two youngest died last week within days of each other, poor things.

Penny wet the tea, not that she'd have time for a mug, and did her best to ignore Billy-the-Beastly.

"Come on, Penny, let's go down to the docks," Billy whined.

"I will not. Anyway, who says that ships crashed into one another?" Penny spooned the last bit of porridge into Maggie's mouth, then wiped her face with a cloth. "Good girl. All gone."

"Must be true." Billy's voice rose to a high-pitched whine. "There's smoke reaching the sky." He grabbed hold of Penny's hand.

"Stop pulling." Penny shook Billy loose and followed him through the parlour and down the hallway.

"Look!" said Billy as he flung open the front door.

Penny stared out into the road. She could hardly believe her eyes! People were standing at windows craning to see down the road to the port, racing down the street to see the collision first-hand, or just standing, arms crossed, tsk-tsking about all them foreign boats running around, bound to crash into each other sooner or latter. Tsk-tsk.

Penny too craned her neck to see the port. A dark column of smoke, with lightning-quick flashes through it, rose up over the buildings. It was down at the harbour all right. Near the Narrows. Papa had his office down there; maybe he was watching the ships too.

"It's nothing to do with us, Billy." Penny tried to pull Billy-the-Brat back into the house, but he would have nothing to do with it. He twisted out

Penny craned her neck to see the port. A dark column of smoke rose up over the buildings. It was down at the harbour all right.

of Penny's grasp just as the paperboy flew past on his bicycle tossing his newspapers every which way. Penny looked down at the the *Herald's* headline: "Germans Start New Offensive to Take Venice."

"Oh honestly, the war. Everything is about the war," Penny huffed.

It was called the Great War, although Penny couldn't see what was so great about it. Not with all the young men coming back on ships from Europe all bandaged up, some with legs and arms missing. Still, the people in Halifax had to make ready for an invasion from the Germans. Why would the Germans want to come to Halifax? Penny's teacher, Mr. Shirley, said that Halifax was a great port, the best natural harbour in the world. Huge convoys of ships gathered in Bedford Basin to make the voyage across the Atlantic. The Germans would like to blow up all the ships that sailed out of Halifax.

"I'm going to go see." Billy made for the gate.

"You'll do no such thing." Penny reached out for him a second time. Too late, he was off. As if his nine-year-old legs were wheels, he sped down the road towards the wharf to see what was what.

"Well!" Penny shook her head. Billy was not her problem, but truth be told, Penny would have liked to have been running right beside him. Maybe she could . . .

"Penny!" Emily cried from the kitchen, "Maggie threw her porridge bowl on the floor and it's all broke!"

"Too hot." Emily set to unbuttoning the buttons on her coat, which Penny had just buttoned.

"Don't," Penny snapped. "It might turn cold later on. And put on your hat and mittens."

Penny poured milk into Maggie's bottle and struggled to attach the dummy. If it wasn't on just right, it would fly off and Maggie would be covered with milk.

"There!" Penny gave the bottle a satisfied shake, wrapped it in a tea towel and tucked it into

Maggie's baby bag. The clock chimed nine. No time for so much as a sip of tea.

It was a chore getting Maggie into her leggings and wool coat.

"Stay still!" Penny tied the hat strings under Maggie's chin and nearly forced her little hands into her mitts. Maggie squirmed. "Outside, Emily. Wait for me in the front by the pram." Penny pulled on her old blue coat and did up the three big buttons. The fur collar that Mama had taken from her own coat brushed her face. The coat was too small, but how could she give up the last thing Mama had made for her? Maybe Mrs. Hanson could help her let it out a bit.

Penny jammed her lunch bag into her pocket alongside her mittens and wool hat, slung her book bag over one shoulder and Maggie's baby bag over the other, then heaved Maggie up on one hip. "Ohhh," she moaned and sagged under the weight.

Maggie arched her back and let out a wail.

"Oh Maggie, stop it!" Penny charged through the house to the front door.

"Look!" Emily stood by the garden gate and pointed to the grey-black billowing smoke that continued to rise in the distance.

"I see it." Penny didn't so much as look in that direction. Instead, she tumbled Maggie onto an old quilt that lay in the bottom of the great pram and tucked it around her.

" 'Fire!' " Emily jumped up and clapped her hands. " 'Fire, fire,' said Mr. McGuire. 'Where, where?' said Mrs. O'Hare. 'Down the town,' said Mr. Brown." Emily clapped her mittened hands and danced as she sang her rhyme.

"Emily, enough!" Penny huffed. "Do you want to ride or walk?" The pram could fit both girls if they didn't wiggle too much. Besides, there was no time for Emily to dawdle. Mrs. Hanson may be only a few doors down, but Emily could turn a short walk into a day's journey.

"I want to go see the fire." Emily stomped about. "I want to see the fire! 'Fire, fire,' said Mr. McGuire. 'Where, where?' said Mrs. O'Hare."

"No! I have to get to school!" Bloomfield

School wasn't far, but at this rate she'd be half an hour late.

Penny scooped up the wriggling Emily in her arms and sat her face to face with Maggie in the pram. Then came the explosion.

The ground pitched and buckled. It rolled as if a giant at the centre of the earth were turning over. Then came the thunder, bigger than thunder, like all the thundering from the beginning of time was rolled up into one mighty crash. And then, as if she were no more than a bit of paper, Penny was lifted up into the air, up and up, and just as suddenly slapped back onto the ground.

Seconds later came the smashing and breaking of glass and the splintering of wood. "Mama," Penny sobbed, and then, "Papa."

She lay flat out on the road, yards from where she had last stood. What was it? What had happened? Had the Germans come? Had the war come to Halifax?

"Maggie. Emily," she whispered.

Her arms and legs would not move, would not obey.

"My eyes," she heard, over and over. Not one voice but ten, a hundred. People calling out, "Help me, my eyes. I'm blind. Help me!"

Penny pulled her legs up and then pushed up on her arms. She rested for a moment on her hands and knees. Up, up. "Emily," she whispered. Time went by. How much?

A black rain began to fall. It was oily and choked her. Penny spat on the ground. There was screaming and the roar of fire and through it she heard whimpering, like the sounds of kittens caught in a trap.

"Maggie, I'm coming." She had to stand, but there was nothing to grab onto, nothing to pull herself up with.

Penny flipped over and thumped down on the hard, surprised ground. Her eyes began to focus. Through the black rain she looked up the street. Where was she? What was this place? Many houses sagged. Every house was windowless. People ran in every direction, their faces streaming with blood, shards of glass sticking out of their heads, their faces, their bodies. Some were naked, their clothes blown away by the explosion.

"Emily! Maggie!" Penny stood and the world seemed to shift. She blinked, tried to focus. *Walk*, she commanded her legs. *Walk*. Her house? Where was her house? There. It was tilted but still standing. The doors and windows had been blown in.

"Billy!" Mrs. Hanson, a big woman who never ran, came running. "Billy? Billy!"

She stopped in front of Penny. "Have you seen my Billy?" she cried.

Who was Billy? She couldn't think. She didn't answer but only stared up at the woman's blackened face.

Mrs. Hanson spun around and ran down the road, screaming her son's name. The next scream came from Penny as she sank to the ground. A piece of glass as big as a plate was sticking out of Mrs. Hanson's back.

CHAPTER N°4

Penny reached up and touched her head.
Blood poured down from a gash above her
eyes. She wiped her forehead with her sleeve
and cocked her head towards the sounds of
whimpering. There! They were coming from
the overturned pram. It was wedged between a
huge piece of wood and the side of the house.
Penny stood on two trembling legs and blun-
dered across the road towards the pram. A crowd
of shell-shocked people were stumbling up from
the harbour. A slight, ten-year-old girl was no

match for the force of fearful people lurching and lumbering towards her. It was as if the road rose up and pulled her back down to the ground. And then something big crashed down on her legs. She scrambled back and pulled her legs to her chest. People were stepping on her! "Oh, oh, get away, away!" Penny flung her arms out in front of her face and batted at the air. "Away, away."

"Zeppelins," someone cried, "German Zeppelins."

"It's the end of the world," howled another. "Repent. It's the end of the world."

Hand over hand Penny crawled towards the pram. Again she stood and lurched forward. "Maggie, Emily, where are you? Please, please God, help me find my sisters. Please."

The pram's large underbelly faced the blackened sky. Its wheels, still attached, spun on their own. A blown-out window frame pinned the pram firmly to the ground and the side of the house. Glass and bits of wood and debris covered everything.

"Emily? Maggie? Please, please be all right." Penny tried to lift the wooden frame. Bits of glass and splinters scored her hands. She dropped it. It was heavy, too heavy.

"Help!" she called out to the street. "Help me, my sisters are under here!" she yelled, and then she tried to lift it again.

"Stand back." A woman, her face hidden by a dark scarf, came up behind Penny.

"I can lift too." Penny lunged forward.

"Back!" the woman commanded, with such force that Penny obeyed.

"Please, please be all right," Penny whispered, her eyes fixed firmly on the upside-down pram.

With a mighty tug, the woman heaved, and then tossed the window frame aside, as if it were nothing, as if she were lifting feathers. As if she had the strength of an angel.

"Thank you, thank you," Penny sobbed. She bent down and, with bloody hands, gently lifted the shell of pram.

Four small, frightened eyes stared back at her. There they were, safe, like two kittens in a lair.

"Penny!" Emily threw herself in her sister's arms. "Bomb. Bomb."

"Yes, my love." Penny held Emily tight as she reached for Maggie. Maggie's eyes were wide with fright but she wasn't crying. Not a sound escaped her lips.

"Put on your gloves," said the woman, "and your hat. They're in your pocket."

"Yes, yes." Penny searched through her pockets and did as she was told. "Thank you." Wait. How did she know that her gloves were in her pocket? Penny turned to look up at the woman. Where did she go? The woman had vanished, as if she had never been there at all!

"Bomb, bomb," Emily cried.

"Oh, Emily." Penny turned her attention back to her sisters and held both girls as tightly as she could.

"I'm sorry that I was cross with you this morning. I'll never be cross with you again. Never." Penny buried her face in Emily's coat. "Maggie." Penny pulled the baby in tight. "It wasn't your fault that Mama died. It wasn't. I didn't mean to blame you. I love you." Penny sobbed as though her heart would break.

Baby Maggie let herself be hugged but did nothing to return it. She didn't blink, not even baby sounds escaped her lips.

A sharp crack sounded. Penny's head snapped back. It was ominous and there was no mistaking it, it came from the house. A beam had broken. She looked up. The house would fall on top of them if they didn't move quickly. Penny scrambled to her feet and turned the pram over. It rocked back and forth for a moment before settling.

A green, horse-drawn, two-wheeled cart, with the word COAL printed on the side, came roaring up the road. "Run," yelled the driver, "there's more to blow. The barracks," he cried. "The fire has reached the Wellington Barracks!" He cracked his whip, and the horse, its eyes wide with fright, reared, then stumbled onward through the debris.

"There are explosives in there," Penny cried. "We have to get out of here. Hurry! Come on, both of you."

With a strength Penny didn't know she had, she hoisted both girls up at once, tossed them into the pram and buried them under the quilt. The baby bag landed on top. Penny turned the pram to face the street.

The crowd on the road moved like a mass. They were heading towards Citadel Hill, the great British fortress that dominated Halifax. How would she get this pram up the hill? The wheels were loppy to begin with and now each one seemed to go in a different direction. With all the strength she could muster, Penny pushed the pram into the crowd and joined the stream of humanity that was charging up the hill.

CHAPTER N° 5

The next few hours passed in a blur.
Penny pushed the pram over broken cobblestones,
around uprooted trees and telephone poles that
had been snapped in half, past churches and
schools that had been hollowed out like sand
castles. Dangling live wires, swinging freely,
crackled and sparked in the air. Fires, some engulf-
ing entire houses, others smouldering, burned on
every side. Penny didn't look back. *Don't look back.*

It was cold, freezing cold. Still, sweat poured
down her face. Penny pushed and shoved the

pram through the hordes of people that moved at a lumbering pace. Bleeding, broken men, women and children stumbled about. Some were being carried on makeshift litters, some in wheelbarrows. She passed soldiers, destined for the front, hauling the wounded across their backs, as though they were already in the trenches. She passed dead people. And Papa, she tried not to think of Papa.

There was talk. "Fifty German U-boats are in the harbour."

Another voice shrieked, "The entire German fleet has landed. It's the invasion of Canada!"

"Papa, please, help us. Papa, please." Penny prayed and pushed, prayed and pushed.

"Make way," hollered a man standing on the running board of an automobile edging its way through the moving crowd. "Make way, ambulance coming through." It wasn't an ambulance, not a real one, but an auto filled with wounded people. It passed so close to Penny that, had the window been down, she could have reached in and touched the driver. And then she recognized him.

"Uncle Robert!" Penny shouted. "Robert!" It was him. It was him! It was Aunt Colleen's brother. "Help!" Penny thumped the window. "It's me, Penny." She let go of the pram's handles and, with both fists now, hammered the side of the auto as it passed. "It's me, Penny. It's me. Stop!" But Robert didn't hear, couldn't hear through the cries and sobs of those around him.

The car inched forward through the crowds. As it moved past, people filled its wake. And then it was gone. Swallowed up.

"Penny!" Emily screamed from inside the pram. "Penny!"

The pram!

"Emmmm!" Penny spun around. The pram was rolling backwards, back down the hill! It became caught in the surging crowd. It twisted and turned around. It rocked with a fury, back and forth.

"No! No!" Penny shrieked as she ran, shoving and pushing. "My sisters! My sisters!" She swung her arms, any way, all ways, hitting anyone. "Let me through." She fell into the path of a wheelbarrow and felt its front wheel ram into her stomach. Penny pulled her legs up and twisted out of its path. The man pushing the wheelbarrow didn't stop, couldn't stop. His two small children lay curled up in the bottom, asleep.

Up again, the pain in her stomach making her stumble in all directions. Where was it? Where did it go? There! Penny ran. The pram had come to rest against a fallen tree.

"Maggie!" Penny ripped back the top of the pram and stared inside. Emily cried out; Maggie, unblinking, just stared ahead.

"Hush, hush," Penny whispered as she bent down and gathered them to her. "Hush, don't cry. We are all right."

Penny looked up. They'd lost ground. Grabbing the handle of the pram, she gave it a mighty shove and once again, started up the hill.

The slopes of Citadel Hill were littered with ragged, damaged, broken people. The crowd grew thicker as she tried to get closer to the walls of the old fortress. They would have to leave the pram behind.

"Emily—" Penny stopped "—you'll have to walk now."

Emily whimpered and snuggled closer to her baby sister.

"Come on, you can do it." Penny scooped Emily out of the pram and set her down on her two wobbly legs. She immediately sank to the ground.

"Come on, you are a big girl. You can do it."

Penny reached back into the pram and pulled out the baby bag. Like a small miracle, the baby bottle inside was unbroken. She flung the bag over her head so that it hung down her back.

"Up you get, Emily. Stand up, you can do it." Emily struggled to stand on her five-year-old legs as Penny reached in and hoisted Maggie into her arms.

The pain in her stomach shot up and Penny staggered under the weight of the one-year-old.

With one arm around Maggie, Penny reached back into the pram, grabbed the quilt and flung it over the baby.

The walls of the Citadel were not far; still, it seemed like miles. Penny stumbled onward, the baby clutching her, Emily holding on to her coattails. "See? We're going up there, beside the wall. Come on." They picked their way through the ash-covered faces. Some huddled together, others sat silently. She could hear bits of prayers, most uttered quietly, some sung to the heavens.

"Our Father, Who art in Heaven . . ."

"But he that trusteth in the Lord, mercy shall compass him about."

And from a clutch of people huddled around a few smouldering sticks, *"in nomine patris, et filii, et spiritus sancti,"* in the name of the Father, and the Son, and of the Holy Ghost.

Grey people wrapped in rags huddled together, warming themselves around a small fire. At last they found a spot against the Citadel wall. Penny spread the quilt out as best she could, sat Maggie and Emily down side by side and tucked the quilt around them.

"Here, Maggie." Penny pulled the baby bottle out of the bag and passed it to her sister. Maggie shoved it in her mouth and sucked. It was then that Penny realized that Maggie hadn't cried, hadn't made a sound since the explosion. "Emily, eat this." Penny plunged her hand into her coat pocket and took out a flattened sandwich. Emily shook her head furiously and then buried herself under the quilt. Well, maybe it was better to save the food they had. Who knew how long they would have to wait for their next meal? Penny shoved the sandwich back into her pocket.

Grey people wrapped in rags
huddled together, warming
themselves around a small fire.
At last they found a spot
near the Citadel wall.

She was so cold. They were all cold. Her fingers and toes were numb. Scrunching and unscrunching them did no good. Penny leaned against the Citadel wall and looked towards the harbour. Boats scooted madly from one place to another looking for survivors that had fallen off ships or been washed into the water. The South End of Halifax looked safe enough, but from this distance she couldn't see the blown-out windows or the havoc. Then Penny turned her face to the North End. It was now a sea of flames and belching black smoke.

Penny covered her blackened face with her blood-crusted hands. "Papa, our home," she cried, her body heaving with sobs, "and my blue dress."

CHAPTER Nº 6

The weather was changing. There was something in the air, a storm maybe. Penny, Maggie and Emily huddled together. Penny could hardly whisper through her chattering teeth and blue, cracked lips.

"Here you go, children." Penny's head snapped up and she stared at a woman who, basket in hand, was giving out packets of biscuits.

"Thank you," Penny whispered. She passed the biscuits to Emily.

Emily screeched.

"What is it? What's wrong?"

Penny looked into Emily's open palm. The biscuits were covered in blood. "Hush, Emily," Penny whispered into her sister's ear. "Hush now. It's just blood. Look, I'll throw it away." Penny took a biscuit from Emily's hand and pitched it down the hill. "See, all gone."

"I'm cold." Emily nibbled at the biscuit.

"I know." Penny wrapped her arms around Emily and pulled her close. "I know."

"All clear!" Soldiers bellowed into megaphones. "All clear." There would be no more explosions. They could go back to their homes now.

"Where are the Germans?" someone shouted.

"What about the invasion?"

The crowd demanded answers.

There were no Germans and there was no invasion. Two ships, one loaded with explosives for the war in Europe, the other bound for New York, had collided. One of them blew up. It was a soldier who said all this in a matter-of-fact voice, but then, he was back from the war and nothing could surprise him now.

"How many?" gasped a woman. "How many dead?"

"Hard to tell," shrugged the soldier, and he began to bellow into his megaphone once again.

Penny scrambled to her feet, skirted a small fire and the people huddled around it, and grabbed hold of the soldier's sleeve.

"My father, he was down at the dock." Penny's voice broke.

"Nothing left standing down there. Wouldn't hold out much hope, miss," the soldier said briskly as he limped away.

Penny carefully picked her way back to her sisters.

A thought, one that had been nibbling at the edge of her mind, now hit her with such force that she crumpled forward.

Papa was dead.

"Come on. We have to go." Penny scooped up Maggie.

"Where?" Emily sobbed. "Where are we going? Penny, where?"

"Home," Penny replied.

With baby Maggie in her arms and Emily clutching her coattail, Penny staggered back down the hill towards Macara Street. The sight of the streets below took Penny's breath away. It was as if a hand of steel had come down and hammered her whole world.

"Don't look, Emily," Penny cried. "Just hold on to me." Penny pressed Maggie's head against her fur collar and hoped the baby was asleep, but Maggie's eyes were wide open, taking in everything.

Penny, too, tried not to look at the lacerated faces, the lost souls staggering around her. And then they were home, or what was left of it. Only the back wall of the house remained standing.

"Gone," Emily cried, "all gone."

Penny sat Emily against the wall and settled Maggie beside her, then tiptoed though the cinder and ash, broken boards, smashed bricks. There were bits of things she recognized, the handle of a cup, hinges from the cupboard, half a book. The clock! Mama's clock! There it was on the floor, its face smashed. Penny seized it.

"What should I do?"

Staggering back to her sisters, Penny huddled beside them and closed her eyes.

"Penny!" The voice was far away, as if in a dream. Penny drifted in and out of sleep. She was back in her own bed, with Maggie tucked in beside her. She was warm. Warm.

"Penny!"

The voice held such urgency, such pain.

"Penny!"

It was fading now. Going farther and farther away.

Her eyes flew open.

Papa! Where was he? Was it him? Had she dreamed it?

"Papa!" Penny struggled to her feet.

"Penny, don't go." Emily, too, awoke.

"Stay here, Emily, stay with Maggie," Penny hollered as she ran, ran after the voice, around the wall and into what was once their street.

"Papa," she wailed. Where was he?

"PAPA!" He wasn't there. "PAPA!"

A ragged man with a face like a coal miner, his clothes a bloody mess and all but torn off him, looked back. His arms had turned blue with the cold. Was it him?

"Papa?"

The man stopped, looked, and then staggered towards her, his arms outstretched long before he reached her. And then he was holding her, his face buried in her hair.

"My girl," he sobbed. "My beautiful Irish girl."

He held her so tightly that the warmth of him spread over her like a blanket. "I thought," he sputtered and stopped. "Your head? Are you hurt?"

"No, no, I'm fine. Oh, Papa." Penny held on to him, tight, tighter.

Papa pulled away. Fear suddenly filled his eyes. "Your sisters?"

"They're fine too, Papa. Look, over there, behind the wall."

Penny felt herself lifted up into the air and carried in his arms as if she were nothing more than a piece of cloud. He fell on his knees in front of his girls and scooped them up, kissing each one. Kissing and hugging. "Thank you." He threw his head back and cried to the open sky. "Thank you."

Emily's tears flowed and mixed with Penny's and Papa's. Only little Maggie remained unmoved, her unblinking eyes just staring up at Papa's blackened face.

"Look." Emily pulled out Mama's broken clock and handed it to Papa. "Penny found it!"

There was nothing more that could surprise

Penny felt herself lifted up into the air and carried in his arms as if she were nothing more than a piece of cloud.

him this day. He took it in hand and laughed, laughed long and loud.

"All broken," said Emily.

"It can be fixed, Emily." Tears slid down Papa's face.

"Papa, a soldier said that down by the harbour everyone was killed." Penny struggled to speak through her own tears and chattering teeth.

"I was out on a job, my darlin'. Safe enough. I've been back here three times searching for you. Oh, my lovely girls. Come on. Shelters are set up around the city. You need to get warm."

"Billy Hanson, Papa, he went down to the harbour . . ." Penny's voice trailed off.

"I haven't seen him, but don't give up hope. Come now." He heaved Maggie and Emily up into his arms.

"What will we do without a house?"

"We'll build a new one, a fine one fit for my angels." Again Papa looked up to the sky, as though he were talking to someone else.

"Does that mean that I won't have to go to Montreal to live?" Penny's words came out in such a rush that she was left breathless with the effort.

"We'll stay together and make do with what the Lord has given us."

"Oh, Papa." Penny leaned against him.

Papa kissed the tops of Emily's and Maggie's heads over and over as he walked, as if he couldn't get enough of them, as if he couldn't believe his blessings. He looked down at Penny, and there was nothing but love in his eyes. "Your mama would be proud of what you have done this day."

ENDNOTE

On December 6, 1917, two ships collided in the narrowest part of Halifax Harbour. One ship, called the Imo, *was heading for New York. The other ship, the* Mont Blanc, *was loaded with a huge stock of highly explosive materials destined for the war.*

Of the more than 65,000 people who lived in Halifax, over 1,900 were killed, although no completely accurate statistics are available. Flying glass blinded 37 people while another 250 eyes had to be removed. Over two and a half kilometres of land around the harbour was completely destroyed. Then fires sprang up. And, as if this weren't enough, the next day a terrible snowstorm blanketed the city. Among the devastation and ruins, Penny and her sisters and thousands of others fought for their lives.

Acknowledgements

Cindy Kantor, who brought the idea for
the series to Penguin.

Barbara Berson, senior editor.

Catherine Marjoribanks, copy editor.

Janet Kitz, writer, historian and brilliant fact checker.

Shannon Proulx, production editor,
patient in the extreme.

D. J. (Ian) McKay, father and fastidious editor.

Katie Parsons, intrepid reader.

Thanks also to Mrs. Aileen Meagher for passing along
her story of the biscuits as retold on page 286.

1608
Samuel de
Champlain
establishes
the first
fortified
trading post
at Quebec.

1759
The British
defeat the
French in
the Battle
of the
Plains of
Abraham.

1812
The United
States
declares war
against
Canada.

1845
The expedition of
Sir John Franklin
to the Arctic ends
when the ship is
frozen in the pack
ice; the fate of its
crew remains a
mystery.

1869
Louis Riel
leads his
Métis
followers in
the Red
River
Rebellion.

1871
British
Columbia
joins
Canada.

1755
The British
expel the
entire French
population
of Acadia
(today's
Maritime
provinces),
sending
them into
exile.

1776
The 13
Colonies
revolt
against
Britain, and
the Loyalists
flee to
Canada.

1837
Calling for
responsible
government, the
Patriotes, following
Louis-Joseph
Papineau, rebel in
Lower Canada;
William Lyon
Mackenzie leads the
uprising in Upper
Canada.

1867
New
Brunswick,
Nova Scotia
and the United
Province of
Canada come
together in
Confederation
to form the
Dominion of
Canada.

1870
Manitoba joins
Canada. The
Northwest
Territories
become an
official
territory of
Canada.

1783
Rachel

Timeline

1885
At Craigellachie, British Columbia, the last spike is driven to complete the building of the Canadian Pacific Railway.

1898
The Yukon Territory becomes an official territory of Canada.

1914
Britain declares war on Germany, and Canada, because of its ties to Britain, is at war too.

1918
As a result of the Wartime Elections Act, the women of Canada are given the right to vote in federal elections.

1873
Prince Edward Island joins Canada.

1896
Gold is discovered on Bonanza Creek, a tributary of the Klondike River.

1905
Alberta and Saskatchewan join Canada.

1917
In the Halifax harbour, two ships collide, causing an explosion that leaves more than 1,600 dead and 9,000 injured.

1896
Emily

1885
Marie-Claire

1917
Penelope

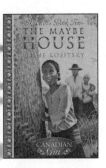

RACHEL: BOOK TWO — THE MAYBE HOUSE

Rachel's wish for a house to call her own is granted, thanks to her stepfather Titan's hard work. And her determination to learn to read and write also begins to bear fruit. But the atmosphere in Shelbourne, Nova Scotia, is increasingly intolerant as delisted white soldiers, unable to find work, begin to look with resentment upon their black neighbours.

ISBN 0-14-331208-1

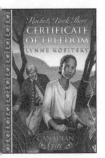

RACHEL: BOOK THREE — CERTIFICATE OF FREEDOM

Racial tension is at a boiling point in Shelbourne, Nova Scotia, as white delisted soldiers become desperate for work. On the pretense of checking their certificates of freedom, one such soldier spirits Rachel and her mother away from their home and sells them back into servitude. Determined to reclaim her freedom, Rachel plots her escape.

ISBN 0-14-301462-5

MARIE-CLAIRE: BOOK TWO — A SEASON OF SORROW

Of the 3,200 people who died during the smallpox epidemic in 1885, 2,500 of them were children under the age of 10. In *A Season of Sorrow*, smallpox descends upon Marie-Claire and her family. How they, their community and the church cope with the epidemic, as well as with the controversial vaccine meant to guard against it, is the focus of this story.

ISBN 0-14-331209-X

MARIE-CLAIRE: BOOK THREE — VISITORS

Marie-Claire is facing the consequences, both good and bad, of her generous offer to house the Linteaus, a family who lost their home in a fire. While their presence fills the house with the vitality and laughter missing since the death of Emilie, it's a small house and there are just too many people living in it. Marie-Claire decides to take matters into her own hands.

ISBN 0-14-301485-4

www.ourcanadiangirl.ca

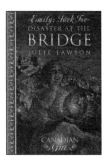

EMILY: BOOK TWO — DISASTER AT THE BRIDGE

Emily Murdoch is looking forward to the four-day celebration of Queen Victoria's birthday. On May 26, Emily, her family and friends climb on board streetcars for the ride to Esquimalt to witness the climax of the holiday celebrations. As Car 16 rolls onto the Point Ellice Bridge, the centre span of the bridge collapses, and the streetcar—packed with more than 120 passengers—plunges into the Gorge.

ISBN 0-14-331206-5

EMILY: BOOK THREE — BUILDING BRIDGES

Hing's family finally arrives and Emily at last meets Mei Yuk, Hing's daughter. After a rocky start, the two girls become fast friends. But as Emily begins to include Mei Yuk in her social life, she finds things changing between her and Alice, her best friend. Inspired by her art teacher, a young Emily Carr, Emily learns the importance of staying true to oneself.

ISBN 0-14-301461-7

PENELOPE: BOOK TWO — THE GLASS CASTLE

In the wake of the Halifax Explosion of 1917, Penny's father must make a tough decision. Faced with the difficulty of finding housing for his three daughters, Papa sends Emily and Maggie to his sister's home in Toronto. Penny, however, must live with Grandmama in Montreal. This decision devastates Penny, as the life she is offered is not what she imagined.

ISBN 0-14-331207-3

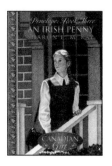

PENELOPE: BOOK THREE — AN IRISH PENNY

The Great War in Europe continues to cast its shadow over the world. Penny's Aunt Colleen is constantly worried about her brother, Robert, who is serving in France, and though Penny is also worried for Uncle Robert, she's facing her own more immediate problems. She's begun school at a posh private academy, where the upper-class girls tease Penny about her poor Irish father.

ISBN 0-14-301464-1

www.ourcanadiangirl.ca

Don't miss your chance to meet all the girls in the Our Canadian Girl series...

ANGELIQUE: BOOK ONE — BUFFALO HUNT

Buffalo Hunt is set in the West, during the waning years of the buffalo hunt. Angelique Dumas is a ten-year-old Métis girl, and this year she gets to be part of the hunt with the grown-ups. It will be hard work, she knows, and she will have lots of important responsibilities. Just how important they are becomes clear on the day Angelique wanders off exploring, and finds herself in the middle of a buffalo stampede.

ISBN 0-14-100271-9

ELIZABETH: BOOK ONE — BLESS THIS HOUSE

When Elizabeth moves with her Planter family from New England to Nova Scotia's Annapolis Valley in 1762, she has a bad feeling about her new home. Elizabeth's family is given a farm that belonged to the Acadians, who have been deported by the English. Elizabeth soon discovers that someone is stealing their eggs and milk. And much worse, the Acadians — who must surely despise all Planters — are imprisoned in the barracks nearby.

ISBN 0-14-100251-4

ELLEN: BOOK ONE — HOBO JUNGLE

It's 1939 and times are tough in Vancouver. Ellen's dad has just lost his job and Ellen and her family have to move across town to stay with her grandfather. Ellen feels so lonely in her new home, and the neighbourhood around her feels unfamiliar. It is not until Ellen meets a new friend and discovers there are people who are much worse off than she that she will learn the true meaning of generosity.

ISBN 0-14-100270-0

www.ourcanadiangirl.ca

IZZIE: BOOK ONE — THE CHRISTMAS THAT ALMOST WASN'T

In December 1940 on the South Shore of Nova Scotia, Izzie Morash, her brother and their friends prepare for a very special Christmas. Despite wartime rationing, and the infrequency of winter visits, the Morash grandparents, aunt, uncle and cousins are coming for Christmas. But plans go awry two days before Christmas, when a huge storm hits the village. Can Izzie figure out a way to save Christmas for everyone?

ISBN 0-14-100272-7

LISA: BOOK ONE — OVERLAND TO CARIBOO

It's the spring of 1862, and an expedition of 150 men is making the perilous journey from Quebec and Ontario to the west coast of Canada, where gold has been discovered. At Fort Garry (now Winnipeg), ten-year-old Lisa, her aunt, uncle and their three young children join the group. As Lisa and her family endure the rugged journey to the goldfields of Cariboo, they encounter terrible hardships — and learn how important they are to one another.

ISBN 0-14-100327-8

MARGIT: BOOK ONE — HOME FREE

As World War II rages in Europe, Margit and her mother are forced to flee their home in Czechoslovakia and seek refuge in Canada. They are Jews, and although life is difficult in this unfamiliar land, they know life would have been much worse had they stayed behind. Although Margit manages to make some new friends, she cannot help wondering what will happen to her when the war ends. Will she and her mother be sent back to Czechoslovakia? And will they ever be able to find her father, who was taken away by the Nazis?

ISBN 0-14-331200-6

www.ourcanadiangirl.ca

Check out the
Our Canadian Girl website

Fun Stuff

- E-cards
- Prizes
- Activities
- Poll

Fan Area

- Guest Book
- Photo Gallery
- Downloadable *Our Canadian Girl* Tea Party Kit

Features on the girls and more!

www.ourcanadiangirl.ca